THE VOICE HEARER

Also by Michael Flavin:

One Small Step

THE VOICE HEARER

Michael Flavin

PRESS

Published by Vulpine Press in the United Kingdom in 2024

ISBN: 978-1-83919-563-1

www.vulpine-press.com

To my wife and children

Thanks to Geraldine Knights and Enda Kenneally, for feedback on early drafts.

Radio. Scramble. Ssshhhhh. White noise.
A voice. Listen to the voice. Despite haze, despite fog...
The voice wants you to hear. It wants you, you, to listen.

'Who's there?'

'Tell me who you are first.'

'You know me.'

'Is it you?'

'Yes.'

'Yes, I did know. I was expecting you.'

'But, but someone else is here.'

'It's OK, I'm a friend.'

'A friend. Are you the one who knows everything?'

'No.'

'But maybe you can help.'

'Do you need me? I don't think there's anything to be afraid of. We are born with the fear of falling and of loud noises. Our fear of falling is why babies grip, cling to their mothers like our simian ancestors. A loud noise meant a threat. All our other fears are learned and can be unlearned. Are you sure you need me? Surely we all know the answers, deep down?

'You are needed... Look there, there.'

I write things down all the time.

An act of writing implies a reader, even if it is only oneself.

But I do not write for myself. I know who I write for, but she is not listening any more.

Dr Robert Field

The first time I saw Harrow he was in his room at the hospital, sitting on his bed. He looked older than forty-one. His
hair was short and dark brown, thinning on top. There was a
scar on his crown. He had deeply ingrained crow's feet
stretching back to his temples and puffy bags underneath his
eyes. He was thin; his veins stood proud of his hands. He
wore his own clothes; a dark blue, V-neck jumper, white shirt
frayed at the collar and black trousers.

I am always closely attuned to the behaviour of a new patient. At least half of them go for mirroring; they copy, sub-
consciously, my gestures. Victor Harrow was not like that.
He looked at me for a few seconds. His eyes were green,
flecked with grey. I stepped forward, introduced myself and
offered a handshake. He accepted but kept his hand close to
his body. His touch was hesitant, even wary. The hand was
cool. He did not stand up. He did not even offer his name
until I said, 'Mr Harrow, I presume,' and we started talking.

Harrow was prosecuted for two counts of manslaughter in
1991. He pleaded guilty on the grounds of diminished re-

sponsibility and was sentenced to indefinite detention in a secure hospital, with a diagnosis of schizophrenia. All the records indicate that, after the first couple of years of his incarceration, he was a model prisoner: library helper; garden supervisor; even an occasional churchgoer.

He was released on parole in 2006, since when he has moved several times and has been a regular outpatient at mental health clinics wherever he has happened to live. He was considered low risk and his regular blood tests (essential for anyone on his cocktail of drugs) had consistently shown a normal white cell count. However, a recent suicide attempt has seen him admitted to my unit. Harrow is still experiencing stomach cramps thanks to an overdose of clozapine, temazepam and over-the-counter painkillers, but his physical condition is not a cause for serious concern. The body will always tend towards self-healing.

Harrow's educational background, which includes a period of postgraduate research, leads me to believe he will find it easier than most to work with my radical treatment. He will be less suspicious than most, I think, and appreciative of a purpose underpinning my approach, a method to the madness. Alongside that, the seriousness of his criminal record makes him a highly suitable case study. If I can get to the root of his problems and offer some relief, I will be able to prove my methods work.

I need to think about which journal I want to use to publish the outcomes and I will need to persuade the Director to fund my travel to an international conference, almost certainly in the States.

The main thing to record about our first meeting this morning is that I gained Harrow's permission to undertake hypnotherapy on him. I should stress that I do not necessarily intend to use hypnotherapy as a form of treatment per se but, instead, as a means of increasing Harrow's confidence in me, and as a means of accessing parts of his self, other than the surface persona. Patients under hypnosis have a heightened level of suggestibility. I may be able to probe gently at his condition and get a first sense of what lies beneath the surface.

As human beings we repress traumatic memories, but if the therapist can return the patient to the state of consciousness they experienced at the time they shut down, they can open the door and hunt down the trauma: in fact it has to be done. Therefore, if I can create the conditions in which Harrow will enter into a schematic programme of psychotherapy, I can hear his whole story and, in the process, address his condition and its fundamental causes. I can also retain the option of using hypnotherapy in explicitly therapeutic ways (as I have in previous cases) if Harrow proves receptive.

I do not publicise my use of hypnotherapy. It just complicates things for medical ethics review panels. It is not a problem. Everyone cuts corners.

The DVD I bought. Real footage, the man said. Two children sitting on the floor in the corner of a darkened room, a dim light shining over them. Hessian sacks over their heads, loosely tied with thick rope at the bottom of each sack. The two of them sitting there with their knees up to their chests.

I hate it when anyone tries to touch me. I lie on my back with my hands at my sides. I look at the ceiling and hold my breath. I imagine I am a seashell or a fossil. No feelings, no life, just a shape drawn into itself.

I stole her sketch book when I left for university. I was flicking through it and noticed holes, like someone had stabbed repeatedly at the pages with a pen. The holes were rough; some of them had not gone all the way through. I had no memory of having done them but it must have been me. Who else was there?

I returned to Harrow's room at four. He went under quickly, after a slow count down from ten to zero. I delivered an established hypnotherapy speech designed to increase confidence. I also tried to find out a bit more about him. Given that he was in a relaxed state and his defences were softened, I thought he might give me some significant first insights. Therefore, while he was still under I gave him a list of colours and asked him to put them in order of preference. He put grey at the top, with striking colours like red and orange at the bottom. His voice was no more than a quiet mumble intoning, 'Grey...white...brown...' I asked him to imagine a box and to open it and describe what he saw. He talked about the inside of the box. No contents; just the inner panels, the floor and the lid.

Some colleagues have mocked my openness to therapies which have not been proven clinically. I trained in hypnotherapy in my own time and at my own expense because I believe there is room for the unorthodox in clinical practice. In fact it is essential in order to push the profession forward. We are too stuck in our ways, too conservative. When I conduct a course of hypnotherapy with a patient I record the sessions and write them up, using the insights to shape patient-specific interventions. My basic method is to conduct five, intensive sessions of hypnotherapy, to expose root causes of mental illness and provoke the trauma into voicing itself. It is not comfortable but it can be effective and it accelerates the treatment. It is like lancing a boil. The pain serves the healing.

I record the sessions covertly. I realise that is problematic, but many of my colleagues and rivals are opposed to radical change on general principle and are sticklers for established procedures. It is a bitchy, back-stabbing profession and there are people out there who would derail my career if they got the slightest chance. They have tried to before. I don't add the sessions to the patient's notes, either.

I also undertook a course in past life regression therapy. I should stress that I do not for one minute believe in past life regression but my disbelief is not the point. The patient's belief in a past life, while doubtless false, creates a stage on which the repressed can perform, thus aiding the psychotherapist. Patients who think they are reliving past experiences are, in fact, acting out aspects of their own trauma in the safer context of historical and psychological costume, like they are putting on a play. They may well believe their experience is authentic, but it is the dramatisation, the projection, of their illness. Alternative talking therapies are therefore most helpful to the psychotherapist. We bring things to life when we speak and when we act. I will use any means to raise a ghost, even if it takes me into grey areas as far as professional ethics are concerned. It is a question of the end justifying the means. My professional expertise kicks in when I expunge the ghost the patient has brought to life through performance. I am like an exorcist.

I suspect Harrow will be grateful for someone to talk to, and (assuming my theory is sound and my preparatory work on him is well-judged) his layers of resistance and sophistry will fall away and he will contribute substantially towards a cure for himself, in the act of understanding his condition and its underlying causes.

Psychotherapists have long recognised the value of silence in treatment. I have taken the next step, maximising the effectiveness of silence by largely absenting the therapist from the interface between the patient and their condition. I steer them into a raw encounter with the repressed. Nothing else will suffice.

My interventions with Harrow will be sparse but well-judged. I will need to hold back as much as possible and allow Harrow to take control of the process and build his own solution by acting out the root cause of his trauma. My first intervention will be absolutely critical. This is hard to explain but, to use a nautical metaphor, it is a question of me subtly pointing the craft in the right direction while allowing the journey to be primarily the patient's. However, it is important that the patient believes they are the one at the helm. That is why I do not pre-ordain a set period of time for my therapy sessions. They can go on for as long as they serve a purpose.

I do not want Harrow to think I have higher wisdom to impart. Psychotherapists are not custodians of the truth. Instead, I want to be Harrow's travelling companion on his journey, doing the manual labour, allowing him to immerse himself in the experience. The discoveries will be all his. I will withdraw into a monitoring, facilitating role, sitting in the room but making sure my chair is the same style and size as his, to symbolise that this is an equal partnership.

I do not use couches. It is what people expect from psychotherapy and for that reason I deliberately steer away from it, though I do position the chairs so that we are not looking at each other directly. I want to guide patients out of their comfort zone, not push them too hard. It can be tempting to do so, but if you push hard the repression pushes back.

It is important to remember that most patients do not want their conditions and neuroses cured; they want them improved. Psychological ailments perform a valuable function for patients, shielding them from the true roots of their traumas which, by definition, they are terrified to face. Freud argued that defence mechanisms are essential. We all repress information provoking powerful negative emotions. I know I do. However, repression creates monsters.

I always present these arguments to students when I am lecturing, in order to get them thinking. I have done a couple of guest lectures for students and early career researchers in Manchester since I got here. I also made it my central point when addressing my team for the first time. I figured them out straight away, eager eyed postdoctoral researchers in their first posts, no job security but with the future laid out before them like an index of possibilities to be accessed at will. They will learn. I scanned the room to get a sense of the ones I can trust and the ones to watch out for.

From my more developed, mid-career perspective, the irrational behaviour traits of patients are most accurately viewed as a means of medicating or managing their trauma. Consequently, my own patients, undertaking my radical therapy, are more likely to say things that are shocking, especially to themselves. The unexpected works. I wrong-foot their defence mechanisms through my seemingly informal approach in which I am more of an absence than a presence, thereby masking the clinical context. My willingness to experiment with unorthodox treatments also catches patients off guard, which is what I need to do to get them to expose their repressed selves.

When I get into the zone with a patient it is like getting them to catch their own shadow. It is like play, but play that is deadly serious. Moreover, encouraging patients to articulate their issues in words makes it less likely they will articulate them through their conduct. It offers an outlet.

My core philosophy is clear: when we speak of a thing we bring it to life and define it. Creating a life is a trauma of its own. However, we need to conjure up the ghost that has been tormenting us in order to lay it to rest finally, at the end. We are both destroyer and preserver.

I will give Harrow the tools and he will hammer out his own treatment. That said, I will also reserve the option of intervention if it becomes necessary, or if a break in the session will stop his ego papering over any of the cracks that might be uncovered.

1st November

I need Harrow to see I am not impregnable, that I have difficulties too and will work with him as a fellow, flawed human being, albeit one without a violent criminal record, to address his problems. Neuroscientists believe that witnessing someone in pain and distress provokes similar reactions to being in pain and distress oneself. Therefore, psychotherapy is dangerous because issues can get transferred from the patient to the therapist. It may seem to follow that experiencing a patient's symptoms makes us, as a profession, more empathetic but, paradoxically, there is a risk that constant exposure to patients' symptoms inures us to suffering. We see so much we cease to care. This is probably one of the reasons why mass slaughter in warfare is common. The perpetrators cauterise their emotions and indeed are trained to do so. Moreover, it is commonplace for murderers and rapists in war to return home and live perfectly ordinary civilian lives. However, emotional reactions to extreme situations do not go away. Instead, and precisely because the emotions are bottled up, they start to ferment.

It is also worth noting that psychotic symptoms occur downstream of the disease. Trauma causes psychotic effects, but not all psychotic effects are caused by trauma, or by trauma alone. There is more to it. There is, moreover, a prodromal phase between initial symptoms and the full out-break. In schizophrenia, for example, the visible onset occurs quite frequently in early adulthood and can be prompted by especially potent life events, but the catalyst can only catalyse because the disease is already in place. If all the component parts are aligned in a particular formation the chain reaction will begin.

Harrow and I were sitting together in a consultation room this morning and he asked me to explain why I was speaking with him. He insisted on a candid answer. I saw no point in lying to him, his crimes notwithstanding. Therefore, I told him I was pioneering a new form of psychoanalytic treatment, combining the insight of traditional psychotherapy with the fast results and coping strategies of Cognitive Behaviour Therapy. I added that I worked in partnership with the patient in a time-limited process designed to reformulate their problems. I told him studies had shown CBT could be effective for halting hallucinatory episodes, but my approach was distinct in offering a long-term solution through short-term, intensive treatment.

Harrow pushed his chair back. He swallowed hard. He looked me firmly in the eye for the first time and said, 'Doctor, I'm not your experiment. You can't use me for your career. I'm not here for you.' He strode out of the room and slammed the door.

A nurse found me later, saying Harrow wanted to see me. I went to his room; he apologised immediately then changed the subject by showing me some of his sketches of the night sky, the hospital gardens and the outline of Manchester city centre as seen from his window. He captures landscape and the effects of shadow very well.

The drawing at the bottom of the pile was different.

'Why have you drawn a closed door?'

'I was looking at a closed door at the time, Doctor. It was the door of the bedsit I lived in.'

'It's good, but most of the page is blank.'

'I know.'

'Why is most of it blank?'

'I ran out of time.'

'Time?'

'Yes, Doctor. Things take time, you know. You can't rush creation. It's ready when it's ready. But eventually something happens.'

'I disagree. Creation can be prompted.'

'You may be right.'

We both carried on staring at the picture. Clean lines, thin but resolute. Like a shape Mondrian was reaching for. A complete work.

I had my own therapy today. Part of continuing professional development. We all have to do it. Her office had a couple of Chagall reprints on the wall. One of them was *Bathsheba*. I looked at the painting, wondering at the mighty King David seeming so small and childlike beside the maternal Bathsheba, kneeling on the ground, burying his face in her lap, lusting for her.

She had Chagall's *Blue Circus* too. I was more familiar with that one. The woman in the middle of the frame was a circus performer upside down, but to me she always looked like a mermaid, especially against the blue background. I could not see a circus artiste, I saw the mermaid instead. Her one, large eye looking out at me and beckoning like a siren's call. In a silence during the session I told the therapist I liked her taste in paintings. 'The room isn't mine,' she said. 'I just borrow it.' More silence.

Eventually, I talked about how I always knew I was going to enter the medical profession. When we were children I would spend hours playing doctors and nurses with Margaret, my sister. I always insisted on being the doctor. It caused fights because she was a little bit older. I always argued we had to do it that way because she was adopted and I was not. The insensitivity and cruelty never struck me at the time. Children are like that.

I fulfilled my ambition but Maggie did not become a nurse. The last I knew she was hairdressing, somewhere in the suburbs. The last communication was a Christmas card I sent her. Not last Christmas but the one before. I just took a card from a packet I'd had for ages and signed it, along with 'love' or 'best wishes.' Had I known it was the last contact I would have with her I would have made more of an effort. I would have tried talking to her in person.

She changed a lot over the years. She moved from place to place. There were a number of relationships. There was one who stuck around for a few years. A businessman, she told me. She never said what business. He worked nights.

Maggie also sought attention. There was trouble over some petty thefts, a few magistrates' court appearances and fines as I recall, but I do not know what happened to her, really. We were not in regular contact. Not regular enough anyway.

Maybe if I had a wife and children I would feel differently, have a different centre of gravity. I would have moved on and I would have had my own family, a wife and a child of my own, but I have always put my career first, for good or ill.

The psychotherapist asked about my self-management. I told her I write my dreams down and self-analyse. I write down other, random thoughts too, which get prompted through writing out the dreams. The practice gives me a different perspective, a sense of myself from the outside. I told her about writing the dreams down but not about the contents of the dreams. She asked me for an example. I made something up, something I knew would come across as the representation of a mundane anxiety about work. She also asked me if I was writing with a particular reader in mind. I said no, because I was lying to her.

I know how to play the therapy game. I know what to hold back. Analysing other people's deepest desires and fears has produced an antipathy in me towards my own. I just lock it all away because I have work to do.

Anais Nin, a writer I always struggled to read, kept a diary where nothing was left out. She recorded every last detail of her thoughts and her sex life. I could never be that unguarded. But she grew that way, she needed the truth likes a rosebush needs soil.

3rd November

I decided not to take my days off this week in order to spend more time with Harrow. I am delighted to record that the investment has paid off. He has warmed to me. He looks pleased when I enter the room.

Earlier today he gave away his own academic background by asking me about my clinical methodology, an act which itself signifies a thawing attitude towards my status and intentions. I outlined my approach and its application. I summarised by telling him that I just wanted him to present his own story in his own words. I also told him it would only happen when he felt that a high level of trust existed between us. He replied, to my surprise, that he wanted to start tomorrow. He also said he thought I was different from the other psychiatrists and psychotherapists with whom he had had dealings in the past. That is normally enough to set off alarm signals in me, as patients who tell you that you are different from the others have generally played the same card several times before on other clinicians. This time, however, I decided to go with it. The potential of this case for my career is too huge to ignore.

There is a risk with starting tomorrow because Harrow will be re-enacting his experiences of extreme violence. It will not be easy, far from it, but he clearly has the desire to purge himself, to tell his own story. His testimony alone will not end his troubles but it will be a significant step, enabling the projection of his condition and its anatomisation, leading to interventions on my part, steering Harrow to recovery.

From my past experience, when patients project their conditions it is almost invariably figurative, at least at first. The analyst has to reverse engineer from the projection in metaphors all the way back to the trauma. That said, we all present ourselves figuratively. We present a face to the world, not the thing itself.

One of the first lectures I wrote was called 'What is insanity?' It was based on Foucault's *Madness and Civilisation* and delivered to first year undergraduate students in a large lecture theatre, the seats sloping up in rows, lots of eager young heads taking notes. I stressed that madness was an evaluative category and had meant different things at different times in western society, having first emerged as a legal rather than medical concept. The way we speak about categories of mental illness, the things we say about particular mental illnesses, are all historically specific and thus subject to change. For example, before the twentieth century much of what we now call mental illness would have been regarded as an hereditary taint, or viewed as possession. The latter could be regarded as demonic but could just as easily be seen as saintly. Moreover, there are communities elsewhere in the world in which people experiencing hallucinations are deemed to be visited by spirits and therefore they do not have a mental illness as far as their society is concerned. The term schizophrenia did not exist before 1911 and we use it to describe a wide range of symptoms, symptoms which are not consistent from case to case. Schizophrenia is characterised by positive symptoms, with auditory hallucinations being quite commonplace, but it is also characterised by negative symptoms including moodiness, poor self-care and social withdrawal, all of which are observable at various times in a much larger section of the population.

Controversially, we can begin to think of mental illness not as something intrinsic but as something we learn, a restructuring of consciousness. We learn to be mentally ill, slotting into the historically available categories. As clinicians, therefore, it may be the case that we medicalise madness through our categories and accompanying treatments but we do not necessarily understand it. We categorise more than we truly analyse.

In the lecture, I asked the students what would happen if they voiced their innermost fears and desires, would others classify them as mad? That always provoked nervous laughter. I asked if they would like to hear my innermost fears and desires. More nervous laughter.

They see me as an established academic and clinician. They do not know what a hard path I had in order to get here. You only get out what you put in: I was told that often enough by my father. It was typical of him – a brusque aphorism for every situation but never a word of encouragement.

I do not talk to students about my past. My persona as it stands gets the job done. But I know what it is like to lose a parent as a child and I know what it is like to do something when you are young that you spend the rest of your life regretting. Maybe that is why I have specialised in working with criminals. It is oddly safe. It has its own parameters, its own codes, like prison life. Furthermore, people who are incarcerated can be exceptionally courteous: they know the incendiary potential of a misspoken word or misplaced gesture. My professional practice means I can deal with issues in a contained way. Everything happens in rooms and cells. I can walk away and know the door will be kept locked. Every individual gets written up in a file arranged by case number and stored securely. Holding Harrow's file in my hand, for example, gives me a sense of control.

I have gone through the pouch at the rear of Harrow's file and found examples of his handwriting. It is untidy. Whole paragraphs are crossed out. He writes about a lot of things but especially about how to find someone. It is noticeable that there are no doodles, just words. I skimmed the first couple of pages but they did not make a lot of sense. The samples of his writing give me a first albeit brief insight into his psyche, but they also give me a feeling of objectivity, of distance. The intellect anaesthetises. That said, I will need a lot more than Harrow's writing to create a solution to his illness.

Harrow's case summaries diagnose him as a schizophrenic and outline how he was plagued by a fictitious character called Gonzago, whose hallucinatory presence was both auditory and, less commonly, visual. This is therefore a good, unusual case, with plenty of substance, not least as schizophrenia itself remains a contested psychiatric concept and label.

But madness and sanity, illness and health; these are points on a continuum, not dichotomies.

11ᵗʰ November

An incredible, breathless week. The full story, no details spared.

I can hardly believe my luck. This is going to be the making of me. It is all there. Get this written up right and I am looking at rapid career acceleration, a professorship at a top university before too long, maybe even the Ivy League in the States, in time.

I have been leaning out of the window, staring at the yellow streetlights across the road and at the multi-coloured lights of the city, the red splays of bars and clubs. I have been listening to night people clipping along the street and laughing. They flock to crowded bars, linking arms, losing themselves in a barrage of light and song after song: *How to save a life, Too little too late.* I can hear the thrum of bass from where I stand at the city's edge.

The night people drink together, clink glasses. They hug. Smiles freeze. I feel far away from their world. They are all so safe, or think they are, not knowing a damn thing about what goes on just the pop of a prosecco cork away from them.

I wish I could tell Maggie about this. It would have given us something to talk about. My career. It got more difficult to talk over time. She became a different person. She got harder, colder. She picked up a lot of behaviour traits from our father, despite being the adopted one. She kept getting into trouble, too, though that's something our father would never have done.

I was outside Charing Cross station at night-time. I was dog tired. The strap of my sports bag dug into my shoulder.

'I can't go on like this darling. You can't keep doing this to me.'

I swear I had never seen her before. She was in her late-thirties and overweight. She wore a short, imitation fur coat and a tight red skirt. I tried to walk on but she grabbed hold of my left arm, her fingers digging in.

'You can't do this to me,' she said.

'I don't know you.'

'Oh don't say that darling.'

People were looking. I shouted 'Fuck off!' and tried to remove her from my arm but she wouldn't let go.

'Joey wants me to sleep with him again. Come with me darling.'

I shook her off and made my way quickly over to the taxi rank. Several drivers were talking together, gathered around the taxi at the head of the queue.

I said loudly, 'This woman has nothing to do with me.'

The taxi driver seemed to accept it.

'Where to?'

'Anywhere.'

'Relationships, eh?'

'Just drive.'

We were still on the cobbled forecourt of the station. The driver was waiting for a gap in the traffic to get away.

Suddenly, the woman in the red skirt was banging at my window.

'I left my bag in there!' she shouted. 'Give me my bag!'

'I haven't got her bag,' I said to the driver.

The driver saw a gap in the traffic and drove away. We left the woman behind.

I looked down at the floor of the cab. There was a small, black handbag. I slipped it into my bag.

Victor Harrow

'Where shall I start, Doctor?'

'Talk a bit about yourself. Your background.'

I was born in winter 1966, in London.

I come from two generations of lawyers. My father worked for his father's firm of solicitors and, when my grandfather died, my father became senior partner, while his younger sister, my aunt, broke with family tradition by working for a charity. She never married.

Alongside my father was the other partner, Malcolm Raynor. He was a widower; I don't know what happened to his wife. In his mid-forties he asked my father to buy him out. Raynor had business plans of his own and wanted the money to fund start-up companies, but he was also an alcoholic and his plans came to nothing. He was declared bankrupt just a few years after the buy-out. My father tried to help. It was a difficult situation because Raynor was either too proud or too ashamed to accept. As it turned out there was not much point in helping because Raynor died of a massive haemorrhage, leaving behind his twenty-five-year-old daughter, Melissa.

My father must have felt a huge sense of responsibility for Melissa. He had always been fond of her and, now that she was alone, he must have felt that he had to take care of her. He paid for everything. A strong bond grew between them. Less than two years after her father's death, my father and Melissa Raynor got married.

My father said he always ignored gossip about the big age gap and just got on with his life. I was certainly a loved child and never sensed any serious tension between my parents. My earliest memory of the two of them is a woodland walk, standing between my mother and father with my hands in the air triumphantly like a sporting hero as I clenched their hands. They swung me through the air at intervals of three steps and I flew freely in the absolute security of their grip. I looked up and the black tresses and curls of my mother's hair in the breeze looked like the threads of a spider's web across the sun. I suppose I was three when that happened, possibly four. I have got memories of my father from what I think was an earlier time, but not my mother.

My parents were well known locally for their charity and it was not surprising when they decided to adopt a child. Maybe there were other reasons for adopting but nothing was ever said to me. My parents liaised with social services and settled on a girl. She was a year older than me. I knew nothing about their plans until the last minute, by which stage it was already a done deal. They told me I was to have a sister, Elizabeth. Her mother had given her up at birth, since when the little girl had been shunted through a series of foster families.

When Elizabeth arrived, a silent, solemn little thing with black hair and large, serious eyes, she may as well have come in a box, gift-wrapped. It was impossible for me as a child not to think of her as a present to play with. Everyone loved Elizabeth.

She and I hardly ever argued. We were always together during the holidays and, though I did well at my boys' school, I was happiest when I was with my sister. In the summer and at Christmas and Easter we were inseparable.

In 1978 my father and mother adopted another child, Jack. He was younger; a toddler. He was small for his age and slim and a constant bundle of activity. We moved to a large, detached house in Kent and I changed schools. It was at school that I met George Gildern, the best friend I ever had.

Meeting George's parents made me realise all families were not like mine. George's father had his own business, a construction firm, no less successful than my father's legal practice. However, Mr Gildern was known for ruling his firm autocratically and he brought his authoritarian streak home with him. You could sense the atmosphere change as soon as he turned up. If we were ever playing out in the street, George would walk indoors as soon as he saw his father's car heading up the road. I would watch him shuffle along with his head down, all self-effacement. Poor George, he could never stand up for himself, right through to the end. As for our family, my parents were not especially sociable and so the five of us spent a lot of time together, but we were content, or maybe you would call it cloistered.

Actually, I think my mother was quite vain. She enjoyed luxury. I remember she owned a fox fur before they became unacceptable. I also remember seeing it draped over her shoulders, the poor creature's forelimbs stretching out like a surrender.

Being one of the bright kids I attracted a bit of stick from my schoolmates but I was pretty adept at blocking out all of the routine abuse. Being good at science got me bracketed as a nerd but I liked other subjects, too. I auditioned for the school production of *Hamlet* but did not get the main part. In a different play, *King Lear* I think, I got cast as The Fool. I died before the end. I also wrote stories in my spare time. George was more of a plodder, a bit part player, but he never minded me being near the top of the class. Then there was Elizabeth, who always joined in whatever we were doing at home. She was no less a friend to George than she was to me, though I was never comfortable if it was just the two of them together. He shared her interest in art and I felt left out when they started talking about paintings.

Elizabeth loved dancing, too, and took lessons, but George and I were united in having no interest in that area.

I watched Elizabeth sometimes, through the crack of the bedroom door. The arch of her back. The unfurl of her arm.

The wrist. The fingers. The pose held. The tight, flat stomach. That sense of total control over your own body.

Elizabeth did not talk a lot. Instead, she danced. When she tilted her head back her neck stretched out and her chin pointed at the sky as if she was provoking it. The air around her began to live.

She never talked about her past, the time before she came to our family. I mentioned it a few times when we were young. I never found out anything. One day my father told me not to ask Elizabeth about her past. I had not done so in front of him. She must have gone to him behind my back.

Harrow paused and took a sip from a glass of water. His voice was clear and well-modulated. His education was evident from his vocabulary and from how his reminiscences were structured. But a psychotherapist is always suspicious of idyllic childhoods because they do not exist. Harrow went back to his story.

I love reminiscing about my childhood. I was happy, secure, shielded from the troubles of the world. However, innocence never lasts, it has to be given up and so I think I can also trace the beginning of my problems to those years.

I had initially accepted Elizabeth and Jack as adoptees, without question and without prejudice. In time, however, and slowly, I began to ask myself questions about my own status. Was I my parents' child? I said it out loud one day and they laughed, but they did not give me an answer. Maybe that was the reason why I started to half-believe in an adult conspiracy, whereby there was a fundamental truth which would decode all the confusion of the world. There would come, I believed, a time, probably a birthday, when I would be initiated in the big secret. My parents would call me into the lounge and ask me to sit down, as they always did when there was something serious to be said. After that moment and the explanation I would be freed from all my anxieties. I had sensed enough about life to realise adolescence was chaotic and I wanted to know what was lying in wait for me. Some of the boys at school already had low voices, marking them out as superior in the changing rooms for Physical Education. It was as though they were branching out into a different species altogether.

He sat back and shut his eyes.

Dr Field

I sat back, too.

Harrow's sense of suspicion and distrust was interesting. He worried that his parents were holding back important information from him. He thought Elizabeth had said something to his father behind his back. In schizophrenia, symptoms are often present some time before the first psychotic episode. It can easily be as long as three years.

In addition, a person's inability to establish and maintain relationships is usually a robust predictor for the development of schizophrenia. It was noteworthy, therefore, that Harrow had only spoken about one friend thus far. It was going to be interesting to see how the relationship developed and to hear about Harrow's role in sustaining it. He said 'right through to the end,' which implies the relationship is over.

It was also noteworthy that Harrow spoke in very short episodes. It was as if he was giving me snippets of his childhood; the edited highlights. His approach might also indicate a tendency to compartmentalise, a strategy for keeping emotions at a distance. Compartmentalisation is also a common strategy for individuals who were traumatised in childhood.

Perhaps Harrow would become more expansive as he went along.

Harrow had mentioned only one detail about his mother; her vanity. By highlighting a fault he was trying to keep her at a distance, too.

Finally, it was clear Harrow experienced anxiety provoked by the presence of adopted siblings in the home. It caused him to question his own identity.

It is something he and I have in common.

Harrow

In my early teens I became hopelessly enthusiastic about the paranormal. I bought Zener cards to hone my telepathic skills, trying to guess each symbol before the card was turned. I read books on every subject related to the paranormal that I could find, from psychokinesis to communication with the dead. I remember my father laughing at me when he found various *Voices from Beyond* books on the shelves in my room. He walked off before I could think of anything to say. I hated him for the first time, hearing his regular, confident steps pad down the stairs. I read even more on the subject as my first gesture of defiance against him. I also decided not to follow in his legal footsteps. But my father was not the kind of man you could rail against. Words never pierced his shield. He never said anything about my refusal to study law. If he was disappointed, he held it in.

I turned fifteen in the spring of 1981. I was not an attractive teenager; my voice was breaking and I was sprouting facial hair. I was not embarrassed by my appearance, though, as I felt I was joining my compatriots who were already swaggering around in their adult male bodies. However, one lunchtime at school I saw something that changed the whole game for me.

One of the tough kids (I forget his name) had long been the stuff of legend for his violent temper. A loud argument had broken out on the playing field and I ran along to watch, drawn to the chaos like motorists slowing down to watch the fallout of an accident. The tough kid had set about another boy, a quiet lad with fair hair. I was part of the dense and baying crowd of boys, swinging back and forth in the melee, staring at the tough kid's red face and his skinhead haircut, the windmill of his arms and the dull thud of his fists against his opponent's face and head. A combination of blows into the boy's mouth and jaw sent his head yanking back at the neck as shards of his front teeth cartwheeled through the air and were pounced on as trophies by bystanders, peeling forth from the crowd and stamping on each other's fingers.

I was transfixed by the fight. I saw the victim's head hit the ground with a graceless thump and bounce off the floor. He had passed out. Silence bleached the crowd. The victor stood there looking clumsy and embarrassed, his arms down at his sides, fists still clenched, his teeth clamped together, his face blood red.

Teachers flooded out of the staff room, barking and yelping contradictory orders at everyone. One of them, a woman, cradled the head of the unconscious boy, his angelic face serene against the patchy grass, blackened and matted with his blood. She held him, craning over his face. I remember his frailness and his stillness. It was nearly perfect.

All of us kept a low profile for days after that as the teachers scowled and snapped at every recollection of our voyeurism. The winner was expelled and a few weeks later a rumour went around that he had been despatched to a psychiatric hospital. The day I heard the news I stopped off at the library after school and took out some books about mental illness. If I had known where my studies would lead me I would never have taken the first step, but there is nothing I can do about that now. A random decision marks the course of your life and you are fixed and fossilised.

The boy who had been beaten came back to school and no one said anything. No one ever said anything. A long time later I read that violence is an attempt to replace shame with self-esteem. I agree.

Harrow stopped.

I was living in a multioccupancy house. I had left my door un-locked and there were men in my room, lolling about, smoking and laughing, pretty much ignoring me when I came in. I went into another room. The man who lived there wasn't in. He had lots of fashionable clothes. I was scared of getting caught if he came back but felt more comfortable in the room with the good clothes than in my room, with all the men.

In 1984, aged eighteen, I was straining at the leash to go to university. I had got a conditional place at St John's College Oxford to read Experimental Psychology, but in the gap between the offer from St John's and the arrival of the results in August I went through my biggest life event to date and began to realise that the world would not effortlessly comply with any plan of mine.

It started with a family crisis. Elizabeth had effectively lost the latter part of 1983 to what we now know as muscular entropy. None of us knew she was developing a serious illness. It crept upon her before pinning her down. At its peak, there were days when she could not get up from her bed, when she could not read a book, open the curtains or, in the worst period, even open her eyes.

She had a poster of Millais's *Ophelia* on her wall and on her bad days she looked like the drowned heroine, lying on her back. It hurt me to see her that way but, to be honest, I think I was also resentful of her cutting herself off from me. Perhaps I was even jealous that she got all of our parents' attention. However, there were also times when I brought her magazines to look at or records to listen to. I liked her dependency on me on those days and did not really want her to get better.

My mother kept a vigil by Elizabeth's bedside throughout her illness. She became obsessive about it. The whole experience was like having a newborn baby in the house. I think my mother liked it that way.

Elizabeth eventually recovered, went back to art college and took up her dance lessons again, but my mother's efforts brought about their own cost. She, too, fell ill, with a dry hacking cough barking out of her lungs sometimes when she tried to speak. She would not go to see the doctor, saying she did not want to waste anyone's time, but when the symptoms got too bad she finally saw our GP. He referred her to the hospital, where her symptoms were serious enough for an exploratory operation.

On the morning she was admitted to hospital my mother left the house in a good mood, saying she would be back in a few days. She was wrong. She had inoperable cancer.

She fell apart quickly, not getting cancer's customary, slow slaughter. Perhaps the speed of the disease was a blessing but it felt as though she knew full well there was no point in fighting. She was soon unable to perform even basic tasks for herself, finding it hard to leave her bedroom, her bones betraying her when she tried to walk. We moved her to a hospice; a grand, old, redbrick building looking out over fields rich with cereal crops. You could see for miles.

The last time I saw her I was with my father. Elizabeth and Jack had not come. My mother was lost in a sandstorm of morphine and could not see me. She did not know I was there. Her skin was yellow as an old church candle. Her cheeks had subsided into pits. She lulled in and out of consciousness, mumbling the odd, incoherent string of words: a prayer recollected from childhood, or a question directed to no one. The pictures on the wall were reproductions of English landscapes showing unfettered fields and easeful skies. One painting directly above her head had a small boat crossing a river.

A combination of her medication and the removal of lymph nodes meant that my mother's right arm had ballooned to two or three times its normal size while the rest of her body was skeletal. She was practically bald. I perched on a seat at the side of the bed, my face level with the swollen arm. It was oddly fascinating. The skin was stretched tight, free of all wrinkles and blemishes.

My father and I left after an hour, by which time my mother had fallen into an unreachable sleep. I was relieved to be going. We did not speak on the drive home. I went to my bedroom as soon as we got back. Five days later, early on a bright and cold Sunday morning, my father came into my bedroom and told me my mother had died in the night. He went downstairs as soon as he had delivered the news.

I had seen my mother on her death bed. I got up from my own bed and dressed for the day.

We buried her the following Wednesday. I held hands with Elizabeth at the graveside. She was thin, cold and bony, her knuckles like a door hinge, her body still waiting to claim back the flesh stripped from her in illness. I knew she blamed herself for what had happened even though there was no cause to.

The priest recited a prayer. He dipped a large brush in holy water. He called my father forward. My father shook the brush over the coffin, four times. The priest looked further back towards me. I came forward, took the brush from my father and flicked water into the grave, twice. Elizabeth and Jack were called forward by the priest and did the same as me. My aunt dropped a religious trinket in there. I heard it slap against the lid of the coffin. We stood around the grave in silence while the priest commended my mother's body to the earth and her soul to a heaven I did not believe in.

At the end of the ceremony I looked around. Some people stared straight ahead or at the ground. Some hung at the back, embarrassed, itching to get back to their normal lives. Some cried. I did not notice my father's reactions.

We drifted back home in a flotilla of funeral cars. One of the undertakers let Jack lean forward and hold the steering wheel while we were still within the cemetery grounds. Jack was thrilled.

We never grieved together. In fact, I do not recall grieving at all. I just wanted to leave. I stopped reading my books about the paranormal. My father retreated to his study and to his bedroom. He invested more time in his work. His legal firm blossomed. Jack got more and more independent, getting himself ready for school and spending more time at friends' houses. He still spoke to Elizabeth but had less and less to do with me or with our father. For a previously close family it was strange how we just fragmented like shards of ice struck from the block. We would have all kept drifting apart irrevocably had it not been for Elizabeth. She did everything possible to keep us together. She kept talking to all of us individually and brought us together when she could. She found new energy in a time of crisis when it was most needed. Rude health flowed back into her skin. The *Ophelia* poster came down. I look back on her at that time with a sense of incredible warmth and fondness. I really loved her.

'Can I take a break now, Doctor?'
    'Yes, sure.'

Dr Field

Some first thoughts –

No mention of formative sexual experiences.

I was struck by the mention of loving Elizabeth. In general he talks very little about love, or about other emotions. His feelings for his adopted sister are clearly quite complicated.

Relatedly, the family seems coldly functional. It does not seem to have been emotionally fulfilling despite Harrow saying they were close. His memories of his mother from his infancy are very limited and partly unfavourable, yet she will have been his primary care giver. Maybe the later trauma of losing his mother caused him to block out memories that might upset him, enabling him to deny that her needed her emotionally. It is a common strategy, outlined in Attachment Theory; emotional neglect tends to make people become either clingy, or else cultivate a hard shell. Harrow was clearly in the latter category though it is worth noting he was not a child, legally, when his mother died.

The narrative slowed down for the latter stages of his mother's illness and her funeral. His repression cracked under the strain at that point. The repressed is repressed but it is never forgotten.

Harrow is at ease most of the time when he speaks. Maybe he enjoys telling the story of his life. He likes performing.

I wonder when the seed of schizophrenia was sown? Significant life events often precede the first psychotic episode but there is no mention of any first symptoms in his account thus far beyond a sense of suspicion and insecurity produced by having adopted children in the house. There is also the issue of a lack of friends. Beyond the figure of George Gildern, his school mates are a nameless mass. The one event he focused on was violent and brutal. I wonder why that left such an impression on him, at the expense of all other incidents? Maybe it was a screen memory, something at the limits of what he could recall but masking a far more significant trauma. He remembered the motherly gesture of a teacher.

Overall, Harrow comes across as emotionally cauterised, evident in his cold description of his mother's death. He shut down. He had to. In general, with schizophrenia, the disease is in place before the symptoms become apparent. Therefore, the analyst has to look for the smallest signs, to get as close to the source as possible. All I have so far is a sense of distance and an inability, or a reluctance, to forge deep relationships.

I thought of my own family today, before things went wrong, when we were little children. The trip round the bay in a boat. The sky white as ash. Can't recall my mother being there. There was a shipwreck, a cargo vessel. It had sunk the previous year and was part of the tour, steering a circle around it. The skipper told us how spilt oil had slowed the waves and had tarred and bound the wings of gulls and cormorants. Now the wreck was part of a day out. I remember the bent metal of the ship's hull, the holes. The corrosion the same shade as the sandstone cliffs. I looked out beyond the bay. The horizon tilted. I wondered if anyone had died when the ship sank. The sea shrugged.

I dream about that scene sometimes. More so, recently.

A dream of a cocoon, adult sized, and someone sitting next to the cocoon, looking on. I thought I was the spectator, but realised it was me inside the cocoon.

Or maybe it was me looking on and someone else in the cocoon, in the shroud.

Harrow

The day I left for Oxford, with top grades across the board for my A levels, I had Elizabeth and George standing with me to say goodbye as my father loaded my bags into the boot of his car.

George was leaving, too. He was heading north to read Business Studies at Liverpool, at his father's insistence. We messed around as the boot was slammed shut but the laughter felt false. I waved out of the window as we drove down the road. George and Elizabeth shrank to trembling dots. They stood close together. I thought momentarily about the two of them. My father accelerated and they were gone.

I had been to interviews at Oxford the previous winter but my first real experience of the colleges, with rusticated stone archways leading through into warm green courtyards, and thick grass bordered by manicured flower beds, gave me a sense of accomplishment before I had even set foot inside a lecture hall. I bedded into university like a plant finding its native soil.

I latched on to one lecturer. He was Dr Waldman, a small man in his fifties who, unlike my father, encouraged my interests at every turn and, at my request, supervised my research work on mental illness and criminality in my final undergraduate year. I spent my days in the Bodleian, the University's library. My father, Elizabeth and Jack seemed many miles away. I was where books and learning mattered most, where I got applause and attention.

Initially, I went to see my family at the end of every term, but by the middle of my second year I was finding reasons to stay in Oxford during the holidays. I got a part-time job in a hotel despite the fact that my father was sending me money and paying the rent on my flat. He wrote me a letter offering to pay for a phone connection, but I wrote back and told him a phone would just be another bill to worry about and there were plenty of phone boxes in town, including one at the bottom of my road. I stayed aware of what was happening because Elizabeth sent regular letters, but the constant stream of news just provided me with further excuses not to pay a visit in person.

I took my finals in May and June 1987 and graduated with first-class honours. I stayed in Oxford and registered as a postgraduate research student. I had a clear plan of how I was going to get my doctorate within four years. I was going to write a thesis on mental illness and its associations with particular forms of violence, supervised by Dr Waldman.

With Oxford accreditation I was able to gain access to psychiatric wards and study patients ethnographically. I witnessed the whole range of madness, from violent tantrums leading to isolation in straightjackets and padded walls, down to the helpless, catatonic ones, curled up foetally in corners. I saw a man who had pulled his own hair out, clumps of it sticking out of the gaps between his fingers as he clenched his fists.

I noted the symptoms and evaluated the underlying causes for each patient, basing my findings on theoretical works and published case studies. I avoided reacting to the human misery in each individual case. The doctors on the wards told me I was good at keeping my professional distance. I gave up my part-time job. I regularly stayed awake until three or four in the morning, reading and note taking, my eyes red and dry.

As a result of my research I became convinced I could adjust patterns of clinical treatment such that violent behaviour could be modified, even quelled, not through drugs which merely pacified the symptoms, but by addressing root causes. This in itself did not represent an innovation but, more specifically, I devised a theory of quantifiable catharsis. I believed I could initiate and control the discharge of trauma in order to allow the patient to move on at optimum speed and with maximum effectiveness. I regarded the mind, like the body, as an efficient mechanism with a natural tendency towards self-healing. The brain is a structure comprising millions of neurons arranged into different circuits. Nerve cells conduct electric currents, passing messages from brain cell to brain cell. If we accept neuroplasticity, which in practice is the capacity of the brain to make anew, we can argue that we can stimulate and nurture neuroplasticity in order to enable the brain to reformulate itself and thus we can engage in more controlled and productive ways with trauma, enabling the individual to re-enter society.

My fundamental reasoning is, I believe, still sound. One of the main problems with trauma is that we do everything in our power to avoid confronting it and so it remains, distilling in our heads, becoming more potent and corrosive. When watching a horror film you are being directed to know that the bad thing is behind the next door. You both want and do not want the door to be opened. In my field there is no such ambiguity: the door must be opened. However, the patient will adopt countless strategies to avoid this option. Trying to force the patient will only harden their opposition. Therefore, they must be directed to want to open the door. The clinical challenge is to invoke that desire, to nurture the will to change. The psychotherapist, therefore, has to create the conditions in which the patient will take that next step. To reach the crucial point, the psychotherapist has to adjust the patient's state of consciousness and lessen their defences. My method was like that of the most highly skilled puppeteer. You do not focus on the strings. You only notice the figure's intricate movements.

I worked incessantly but am no longer willing or indeed able to publish my findings. My work lacks the precision that I strove for. Furthermore, the police and psychiatrists subsequently took my research from me. I was a threat to them and they snuffed me out.

The core problem is that people want to have the values of their own epoch reaffirmed. I am a teacher and people hate to be taught. They want to be told what they already know. It is reassuring to them. My error of etiquette was that I challenged their values. They decided they preferred ignorance and crushed the physician.

Back at the original point of experimentation and discovery, however, I did not expect anything other than praise for my work. I had decided to write up my findings and was making progress towards the completed thesis in summer 1990 when odd things started to happen. It troubled me. People like me do not like the unexplained. We insist upon an empirical reason for everything. This was different.

I need to take a break now, Doctor.

Dr Field

Harrow practised reaction formation, exemplified by his not touching upon any formative sexual experiences. Everything got channelled into the intellect and he was clearly more at ease talking about his research than about feelings, which got scrubbed from his account wherever possible. He avoided going deeply into what he felt about the death of his mother (ironic, in view of his theory of trauma) and had little to say about his sister's illness, other than summarising the symptoms. The analysis of underlying causes was perfunctory. In addition, he did not touch on the possibility that his sister's muscular entropy could have had a psychological origin which, in my view, is almost certainly the case. Freud argues that desire, jealousy, rivalry and threat are all key features of the family beneath the veneer of succour and support, but this family, as Harrow describes it, just retreated into solitude and cold politeness in the face of a bereavement. The trauma was placed on ice. It seems the feelings were too dangerous, too febrile, and therefore they were repressed. However, repression is problematic because it just stores up problems for later. Some form of release, some sublimation, is necessary in order to avoid the repressed emotion fermenting and festering. Maybe Harrow undertook some sublimation through Dr Waldman, the replacement father figure, who comes across as encouraging, far removed from the coldness of Harrow's father, though Dr Waldman is also small and unthreatening. Harrow's experiences at Oxford also expose self-centredness and insecurity. He wanted praise and attention. He appeared to have no notable social networks.

My father was cold too, and disapproved of me having friends in the house, and so I stopped bringing anyone home. I know my colleagues find me cold. I have nothing to do with them outside work. And I have stayed single. I used to holiday alone in the Far East. I have stopped all that now.

Harrow uses his intellect as a shield or as a screen to mask emotions he cannot manage. Consequently, he has an analysis of trauma but does not dare apply it to himself. Everything is about the surface or, at best, a cold plateau, an ice shelf from which he can view events at a distance. His academic work fits this analysis because he remains emotionally aloof despite the challenging nature of what he was witnessing in psychiatric wards. His research examined violence. The brutal, elemental world always looked over the shoulder of his intellect.

Another thing: Harrow edits. He cut from his mother's death straight to the funeral. Nothing about the days in-between. I have noticed how adults make themselves very busy after a death. Jobs and routines keep their minds away from the loss and the grieving. It is more difficult for children. They do not have the consoling intricacies of work and paying the bills. Children come face to face with the abyss and shut down.

My story is like Harrow's in that regard and his theory of trauma is, in is rudiments, reminiscent of my own experience. His family structure was similar to mine. The presence of an adopted sibling can cause role confusion. I know that from first-hand experience in relation to my sister, Margaret. But I was twelve when my mother died and Harrow was eighteen. His absolute shutdown on the subject is noteworthy, given that he was legally no longer a child and given that he is clearly thoughtful and intelligent in general. Harrow has more to say but he is not yet ready to say it. He is not opening up to me to the degree he will need to in order to move on. That is OK, for now. Patience will be key to success in this case, but once I get a route in I can open him up.

Harrow's theory of trauma and its treatment is interesting but it is also full of holes. How do we stimulate and nurture neuroplasticity? Harrow is very articulate when he talks about his research but it is as if he is performing. I cannot be sure he is telling me the truth.

A final point: Harrow did not want a phone in his flat. He wanted, unconsciously, to cut the family off. He did not want a symbolic umbilical cord linking him to them. The family had become its own site of trauma, not succour.

His increasing social withdrawal, giving up his job for example, is another classic marker for schizophrenia. It will be interesting to hear his description of his symptoms as they first emerged. He is dating the onset as 1990, six years after his mother's death, but I suspect there were subtle symptoms present before 1990.

We began again. I asked him about the odd things that had started to happen.

Harrow

It was just a feeling of disquiet at first, the kind you get when you have done something wrong and your conscience will not leave you alone. After a week or so a more definite sense of unease began to follow me around college. I felt all my secrets were on display and visible to everyone. A stranger's casual glance would become a deep scrutiny of my face. I started to believe people could read my thoughts. In my more rational moments I put it down to stress and assured myself it would ease off once I had completed my thesis.

My sleeping patterns became even more disturbed. I was used to getting by on small amounts of sleep but this was different. I tried to finish my work earlier in the evening and go to bed well before midnight but I would wake up between two and three in the morning, completely alert. After the first few occasions when it happened I became resigned to the fact that sleep would not return and started working in the small hours, riveted in front of my Amstrad computer screen. In the afternoons I would fall asleep, sometimes deeply but often only dozing, waking again in the early evening. I lost track of time. I started to look haggard.

I went to the doctor and talked about the stress and the sleeplessness but not about people being able to read my thoughts. He prescribed sleeping pills. I tried not to take them too often, scared I would develop a dependency. When I did take the pills I was poleaxed and, though I slept, it only made the other nights, the sleepless ones, lonelier than ever.

The rest of summer 1990 passed in this way, the heat of the long days compounding a series of headaches, threatening to bring all my work to a standstill. Oxford had ground down to slow pedestrians and snarling cars. Tempers frayed everywhere. The headaches forced me to lie on my bed with my eyes closed and the curtains drawn. Even music aggravated my symptoms so I lay there in silence. The shouts of children playing in the street below sounded like war cries.

I avoided further visits to the doctor, knowing he would tell me to slow down and not work so hard, something I was not prepared to do. Instead, I forced myself to keep going through the pain and exhaustion, working whenever I was able. I stopped talking to people at college and I stopped contacting anybody by letter or telephone. Elizabeth continued to write but I sent only the briefest replies as infrequently as possible, jotting down a couple of sentences on the back of a randomly chosen picture postcard, assuring everyone at home that I was all right, working hard and too busy to write more.

Summer gave way to autumn. The air got colder; the wind rose up. The life of the year was being swept away but no one else seemed to notice, insulated in their cars and their double-glazed homes. Only Oxford's tramps knew, wiser in their way than the students and tourists from whom they begged crumbs. Winter was on its way.

My health was at rock bottom. I went from one bout of cold to another. However, and although I was sick, I knew my work was going to be extraordinary. I was on the threshold of a great discovery. I knew it would not be long.

That was when the whispers started.

'The whispers?'

'Really close. It started as a "G" sound. That was all. A voice whispering from the back of its throat: "G." Someone standing behind me, a man, mouthing the sound.

'In mid-November the whispers got longer. There was a full word: "Gone."

'There was no pattern to it. I could be at home or walking the street. The voice would sidle over my shoulder and whisper, "Gone." If I turned round there was no one there.'

'Can you say more about the voice?'

'No, not now.'

'Why not?'

'Because things got worse.'

Harrow put his face in his hands.

Dr Field

Symptoms:

Suspicion and distrust. The emergence of paranoia.

Social withdrawal.

The whispers. Auditory hallucinations. The negative symptoms of schizophrenia become positive at this point. It is a key moment in the progress of the disease.

The voice Harrow hears is characterful. It is not a babble, not a number of voices, just the one.

Causes:

Proximate cause: stress, brought about by high expectations.

More fundamental causes: the Harrow family. The death of his mother. The way the family members all drifted apart and atomised afterwards. The way Harrow blocks off his emotions.

He talks about his conscience. Conscience is a feeling. It trespassed on his cold compartmentalisation of the world. It catalysed the voice.

I am interested in what the voice does, too. The 'g' sound, and then 'gone.' I do not know much about children, but I believe 'gone' arrives early in children's vocabularies, and maybe the 'g' sound is one of the first they master. Harrow's imagined voice is like a baby learning to speak. But the word, gone, speaks of Harrow's loss, the loss he tried to repress.

A dream of a head eating a body. The body tied up in a sack.

Harrow

One night changed my life.

It was late-November 1990. The wind spat rain at my window. It had been falling since afternoon and showed no sign of stopping. However, despite the tightening stranglehold of short days and bad weather I was feeling better because I was about to make a major breakthrough.

I was sitting down in front of my computer. Several days' worth of notes lay on the floor to the left and right of my desk, forming a horseshoe. I was on the verge of formularising a new link between mental illness and violence, unfolding a fundamental template for future analysis and treatment. I was all set to commit my ideas to paper. I was looking, aside from the formula, for the one phrase or sentence which would encapsulate my argument – my own 'survival of the fittest.' Imagine, Darwin's years of research boiled down into a few words that someone else wrote. This time it would be different. The epigraph for my work would be my creation and would establish my name and reputation, maybe even beyond my own lifetime.

Having written down a couple of preliminary sentences I pressed 'print,' feeling certain that looking at words on a page, rather than a screen, would be the final prompt I needed.

There was a knock at the door. Four quick taps.

A random image of childhood, a screen memory, flashed through my head – my father tipping me accidentally out of my buggy, toppling me headlong onto the concrete of our garden path.

'Who is it?'

'Just open the door please.' A calm, quiet voice. It was the same voice that had been whispering to me.

I grabbed the handle and yanked it open. The man standing there in the frame of the door was my age and my height. His eyes were like mine. He raised his right hand and handed me a piece of A4 paper.

'Read this,' he said, in the same, quiet tone. He stepped back into the unlit hall, pulling the door towards him and closing it.

I could not move.

The rain had stopped.

The wind held its breath.

Slowly, I lifted the paper to my face.

Victor. You were adopted as well. Meet me tomorrow at nine a.m. in the courtyard of the Bodleian library and I will explain everything.

My hands shook. The paper squirmed away and glided to the floor. It rubbed itself against the outstep of my feet as it settled, like an ingratiating puppy. I pulled open the door but the hall was empty. I ran down the stairs. There was no one around. The front door was shut. I went back to my flat and stood still.

The ground slipped away as I tried to stay upright. I stumbled to my bed and sat down, breathing heavily. I got up and scrambled to the window, flinging it up and gasping into the cold night until my fingertips were numb, clenched against the windowsill, my head full of white noise. The voice in my head rasped, 'You must stop all this. Must stop all this. Must stop it now.' The same voice but harsher, more imperative.

I closed the window, reached for the bottle of sleeping pills next to my bed and poured them into my hand. I rammed the pills into my mouth and swallowed hard. Some of them stuck against the roof of my mouth or lodged in the back of my throat. I hurried to the sink, poured a cup of water and gulped it down, flushing the pills into my stomach. I reached up to the cupboard above the sink and pulled down a box of extra-strength painkillers. I took them all. I went back to my bed and lay down on my side. I brought my knees up to my chest.

I lay there for three days, hauling myself into brief bouts of hazy consciousness. I craved a drink, gulping straight from the tap, the freezing water shocking my throat and stomach. I felt like a sword swallower, the cold rush of water racing along the inside of my neck.

Each time my thirst was satisfied I fell back into bed. The stomach pains would start within an hour, cramps gripping my guts. I retched up the water into the sink when the pulse of pain grew too strong. The vomit was speckled with the meagre contents of my stomach. It felt like I spat up every drop of my insides.

Throw up. Fall back into bed. Stomach cramps. Again and again. The cloying sheets grabbed at my arms and legs.

I dreamt I was back at home. I was upstairs in one of the bedrooms. I looked in a wardrobe. It contained some of Elizabeth's clothes and some of mine. They were past their best. I just stared at them.

There was a knock at the door, jolting me, and I knew it had to be her. She said she was staying in Oxford for a few days and asked if it would be OK to stop with me. I took her by the hand and pulled her in. I looked out of the window and the street had changed. Instead of the tree-lined avenue I saw a bare pathway. A gang of kids stalked along it, a row of bobbing silhouettes, their mouths flinging curses into the air. I pointed them out to Elizabeth and said we had better stick together.

We fell into each other. It seemed natural, not obscene. I lay on top of her and drew my hand back through her hair. I felt long tresses but Elizabeth's hair was short. I switched on the lamp at the side of the bed and a pyramid of light appeared in the room. My mother lay beneath me, her thighs against my thighs, her neck and shoulders a bag of bones, the right arm still swollen and her face a cold, wrinkled mask of grey-white, arid clay, skin shrivelling to ash. Her hair came off in my hands, black tresses binding my fingers. Her flesh was sliced away in a crescent from her cheek. The edge of her jawbone jabbed into me. Her fingers clutched at my arms, nails digging in, desperate not to be dragged away. Her eyes sprang open, all bare white with no pupils. A soft noise, her stomach beneath me ripping open, the dewy guts billowing out like hot blossom, spilling onto my flesh.

There was a pummelling knock at the front door and I sprang awake in harsh daylight. This time I raced down to the door and pulled it open. There stood George Gildern. I shook his hand. It was firm, real and warm to the touch. He apologised for calling unannounced, said he was visiting Oxford for a couple of days and asked if it would be OK to stop with me.

'Let's go out,' I said, grabbing a coat. I put my watch on. It was almost mid-day.

'What day is it?' I called to George.

'Friday, of course,' he said, looking at me. 'Don't you know that, Victor?'

'I've been busy.'

'Are you OK?'

'Absolutely.'

'Are you sure, Victor? Do you want to change into clean clothes?'

'Come on, I want to go out.'

I led the way, walking quickly, George lolloping along, struggling to keep up and trying to start a conversation. I took him to the King's Arms, across from the Bodleian. I chose a small, round table in the corner from which I could see most of the courtyard. There was no one there that I recognised. I was afraid to go any closer.

George ordered a chicken sandwich from the food counter. I had no appetite. We drank beer together. The warmth tumbled into my stomach, calming me for the first time in days. I did not tell him about my visitor, I did not tell him about my letter. I kept glancing over at the Bodleian, an act which began to attract George's attention as he, too, started looking in the same direction. To distract him, I asked about my family, especially Elizabeth. George said he had called on them the last time he was at home. He admonished me gently for not keeping in touch with them enough.

'You could contact them more frequently, you know.'

'I know.'

'They worry about you, Victor.'

'I know.'

'They only want—'

'Can we drop this now please?'

I looked out of the window again while George toyed with his beer mat.

After a couple of hours and a few more drinks, George asked to go back to my flat. I was drunk by now but did not want to leave the sanctuary of the pub. I wondered how I would feel about seeing the note again.

I felt weak and unsteady as we walked out of town. I thought I might throw up. I tried to put it down to the alcohol and my poor health. I knew there were other reasons for the shivers that gripped me but did all I could to suppress them.

My agitation became obvious as we turned right off the main road and into my street. George asked me what was wrong. I tried to reassure him but it was obvious he was concerned. He put his hand on my shoulder. I shrugged him off.

It was mid-afternoon and the street was at its quietest. I opened the front door. The foyer and the hall were deserted. We climbed the stairs. I turned the key and walked in, raising my right arm to stop George going ahead of me. It was the usual mess: scrunched up balls of paper everywhere, clothes strewn on the floor. I looked in my wardrobe and under my bed. I went into my small kitchen and the bathroom. There was nothing untoward, though I had left my kitchen window open. I stuck my head out. The rusty iron fire escape was over to my right; the next house to my left. I came back in to the living room. There was nothing anywhere to indicate that anything dramatic had happened. I could not see the note.

George watched me as I paced through the flat, inspecting every space I could find. 'What's wrong?' he asked. I turned and faced him and the truth hit me. I had got it all wrong. I had obviously been very ill and, in a hallucinogenic state, I had had a vivid dream of a night-time visitor who looked just like me. I had been unable to disentangle dreams from reality in my weakened state and I had over-reacted chronically by taking an overdose, leading to another hallucinogenic experience involving Elizabeth. The whispers, the man at the door, Elizabeth in my bed: none of it was real. The relief washed over me like a clean and beautiful wave, making me laugh loudly. I laughed like I had not done for years. I felt dizzy, from giggling, from the lack of food and from the lunchtime session in the pub. George grabbed my arm. I let him lead me to my bed.

It took me a long time to get better. The sickness had crept up on me and had possessed me long before I even knew it was there. George was my saviour. He extended his stay. He phoned my family and assured them I would be OK and there was no need for them to come to Oxford. He spoke to them regularly. He cleaned my flat, took my clothes to the launderette and put all the scrunched up papers in the rubbish bins outside. He was my twenty-four hour a day carer.

George went home for Christmas and back to work for his father but I stayed in Oxford to focus on my recovery. I did not want any excitement, I needed calm and silence. I telephoned home to say that I wanted to stay where I was and my father, reluctantly, gave in to my wishes.

It was the following spring, March 1991, before I felt completely normal. There were no more hallucinations and the whispering voice had gone, but I only knew I was fully restored when I was able to walk into town, down the steps at the bridge and along the riverbank to the Isis Tavern and back again without any twinges of anxiety. I knew, too, that it was time to return to my research and complete my thesis.

I had not sat down in front of my computer for four months. I switched it on and listened to the machine's confident whirr revving up before flicking on the monitor and waiting for the opening screen to appear.

George had bought me a gift from an antique shop before he had left; a glazed, plaster model of a human head with a phrenological grid mapped out across it. I kept it on top of the monitor. Individuality lay between the eyes, above it Eventuality. Benevolence was on the crown, flanked on either side by Spirituality. Destructiveness sat above each ear. I touched my own head at the side. I thought there was a lump at that spot. I had never noticed it before. I wondered if my hippocampus was swelling up. I stared at the plaster face and it stared back. I could not work. I switched off the machine.

I wanted, more than anything else, to repay George for his kindness. He had given up his time for me; now I wanted to do something for him. I wrote him a brief note and suggested we go on a walking and camping holiday together to celebrate my recovery. I knew he had seen me at my worst and I wanted him to see the best of me again. I outlined a basic plan, whereby we would meet up in London, make our way to Liverpool St Station and head to East Anglia. I walked out to the post box feeling upbeat for the first time in a long time. The elderflowers were blooming. Fortune was beginning to favour me again.

Harrow's voice changes. He addresses me directly.

'Can I show you something, Doctor?'

'What is it?'

'A letter I received from Elizabeth, a long time ago. I keep it with me.'

'Do you want me to read it?'

'Yes.'

He hands it over. It is still in its envelope. I shudder slightly, remembering another letter.

Harrow's letter is creased, visibly ageing.

Dear Victor,

I have been so worried about you. George has told me every-thing. He has spent a lot of time with us, a lot of time talking to Dad. They have become very close. The last thing I want to do right now is to add to your stress but I would give anything just to get a letter from you, to let us know how you are feeling and if you are recovering.

We haven't heard from you since before Christmas. You ha-ven't written. Can't you go to a phone box and call us, just once a week? I have waited to hear from you for so long. I didn't know anything about your illness until George got in touch. I was wor-ried that something might have happened to make you cut your-self off from us. I'm so grateful to George for all he has done. He is wonderful. Say thank you to him, from me.

Just one call or a letter, please Victor, to let us know ~~if~~ that you are better.

It seems a bit trivial to talk about what's been happening here when you've been so ill, but it would probably be even stranger not to include it, so here goes…We are all well. I'm still at art college and still doing dancing lessons. My group put on a per-formance before Christmas. The local newspaper came with a photographer. They published a picture of me.

Jack is growing so fast. You have really missed out by not be-ing here. It is just great fun having him around and watching him grow up. He left primary school in the summer and is now at the local grammar. He's a slim boy and not as tall as his friends, but he's an absolute angel. He's guaranteed to break hearts when he's older. Just being with Jack or looking at him is enough to cheer me up. Sometimes I get really upset when I think about Mum.

We also have an au pair who helps a lot with Jack, and in fact with everything else. It was Dad's idea and I'm glad he did it. Her name is Katarina. She is from Czechoslovakia. She was very quiet in the house at first, but now she is becoming more confident and Jack adores her. She cooks his tea, does all the washing and helps Jack with his homework. You can tell how important she is at home because, when Jack is upset in any way, he often turns to Katarina rather than to Dad or me. She's really brought the family back together again. We're talking to each other. Dad seems happier than he has in a long time. He spends less time locked away in his study. He takes more care of his appearance at home. He opens a bottle of good wine in the evenings.

Katarina has told us both of her parents are dead. That's terrible at such a young age. Maybe she wants to settle here permanently.

Lots of other things have happened but I suppose that covers all of the most important and basic stuff. We would love to hear from you. A letter, a phone call, a postcard, anything. We would come down but I get the feeling you would probably prefer to be left alone. Do thank George for me from the heart and please get in touch as soon as you can.

With love,
Elizabeth.

'What do you think?'

'I think your sister must have cared a lot for you. Do you keep other letters?'

'No, just this one.'

'Why?'

'It started something off.'

'Meaning?'

'Some things went wrong after that. I sometimes think of the letter as a curse.'

'A curse?'

Silence.

'Do you want to talk about it, Victor?'

'The au— No, not now, Doctor.'

Dr Field

It was encouraging to see some self-awareness in Harrow. He acknowledged that his psychotic symptoms were hallucinations, at least as far as the night-time visitor was concerned. He also seemed to accept that his illness had been in place before the symptoms manifested. However, and in common with everything Harrow had said thus far, it felt like he was giving himself wriggle room, that he could change back again, or that he was only giving me an edited view of events. That is not uncommon, people fictionalise their lives, but I needed more from Harrow to validate my theory and treatment programme and to give him a coping strategy should the hallucinations return.

It was also interesting to witness Harrow's immersion in his story, down to using different voices. I can see why he enjoyed drama at school. It is all one long performance from him. I think part of him craves the limelight.

Harrow's grandiose perception of his own work and its importance ticked the schizophrenia box well enough but other things were not falling into place so easily. Visual hallucinations are markedly less common in schizophrenia than auditory hallucinations. In this case they signify a further and notable stage in the progress of the disease. As for what he saw, it was clear to me that he was seeing himself in the doorway of his flat, though he did not recognise the possibility. Either that or he did not want to talk about it, despite its being obvious.

The note he claimed to have received from his visual hallucination was interesting, too. It could simply have been another hallucination, but it would involve hallucinating the sense of touch as well as sight. I have never heard of that before. A more interesting possibility was that he had unconsciously written the note himself. He was working at a computer, he had his own printer, there was paper everywhere in his flat. It was therefore possible he was unconsciously articulating his suspicion that he, too, was adopted. He was, I think, auto-writing on his computer screen. I have checked Harrow's file notes; he was not adopted. However, for Harrow, it was significant that his parents did not give a direct answer when he asked them the question.

Harrow talked about a nightmare he had had, when Elizabeth turned into his mother. The obvious analysis is that it is an oedipal fantasy but the culmination of the nightmare is bizarre, featuring his mother in a kind of caesarean birth. I do not know what to make of it.

More broadly, the severe symptoms Harrow experienced were very far downstream of his most stressful life events, making it hard to demonstrate a causal link. It is true to say that behavioural and social changes can be observed several years before the first psychotic episode in schizophrenia, but it does not make my job any easier. I intend claiming I can cure deep-rooted conditions in weeks rather than years. At the moment I just have to listen, but my follow up will need to be good. I need to think about my first intervention.

I have my own fears, my own problems. I had an inertia problem before and cannot allow it to happen again. Day after day I just walked down to the sea's edge and watched the cold winter tide seep its way forward. I wondered what it felt like to fall into the sea in winter, not at the water's edge but out there, in the depths, alone.

Harrow had kept a letter he had received from his sister. He placed particular significance on the letter. I could not be certain, however, that his keeping it was directly related to his illness. It is commonplace to give high symbolic value to objects. I keep a letter, too. My own sister wrote it. Harrow talked about his letter being a curse. I see what he means.

I cannot let my personal and professional standards slip. I must stay engaged. I must look after myself a bit better, too, and spend less time alone. Maybe I should talk to colleagues but I cannot trust them not to steal my ideas. It is like every other profession, with everyone trying to be top dog.

Another dream of a cocoon. The life inside it growing, slowly.

Harrow

Later that evening I wrote Elizabeth a brief reply, which I posted the following day. I cannot remember what I wrote to her. I did think about the au pair, though. She might be sleeping in my bedroom.

I wondered why Elizabeth needed to thank George from the heart and why the newspaper published a photograph of her out of all the dancers. I also visited Dr Waldman to arrange a further extension for the submission of my thesis.

George and I spent two happy weeks away together. My physical recovery was already complete and, with George to encourage me, my mind too fell fully into place. I slowed down. I regained my sense of mental balance and order.

I loved the walking. The long, flat expanses of countryside across Norfolk, the landscape and horizon melding, the network of rivers linking everything like veins. I liked the East Anglian towns too. The milling of people through markets or the slow steps of tourists around churches, shifting from spot to spot like shoals of tropical fish.

The camping was good fun as well. We each had our own tent which gave us a little privacy and head space at the end of each day, but we agreed that on the last night we would stay in a double room at the Maid's Head Hotel in Norwich, cheaper than getting two rooms, and spend the evening just drinking and relaxing. We had made a reservation and everything was in hand.

Over the second week I went on some trips by myself. George accepted my reason for my apparently anti-social behaviour, namely that I wanted to discover just how complete my recovery had been by seeing if I could cope without help from him or anyone else. He was happy enough. He had brought his binoculars and went bird watching. I had not known that was one of his hobbies but the binoculars looked like they were new and top of the range. I asked him where he had got them from. He said he could not remember. One day I saw him posting a letter. He had not known I was watching him. I asked him about it later. He seemed surprised at my question and said the letter was to his father. He was finding it hard to maintain eye contact as he said it. I began to have suspicions about him.

I enjoyed my time alone. I reconnected with my old sense of liberation and potential. I felt like a baby taking its first steps. I even went swimming naked in a river when I was sure there was no one else around. Now there could be no doubt: things were definitely looking up for me again.

On the last full day of the holiday, George and I met up outside the station in the late afternoon. We walked over the road to the hotel. The receptionist took our names, reached under the desk and handed me a piece of paper. It was a one-day-old message to the effect that I had to contact my father immediately. I went to the pay phone in the hotel lobby.

I can still recall the icy stillness with which my father said, 'I have bad news for you. Prepare yourself. Jack is dead.'

My first reaction was a paralysing flash of *déjà vu*, the sense that I had always known this moment would happen. I believe a traumatic event can jolt the senses in that way. While I stuttered, my father begged me to come back home, telling me Elizabeth was almost hysterical.

I tried to contain myself and asked what had happened. My father told me Jack had been swimming in a river a few miles away, a place I knew well. Katarina was with him but was not swimming herself. He had swum out of her sight and must have got into difficulty. He probably over-reached himself, or got cramp, or got caught up in an unexpectedly strong current, or else became entangled in weeds or some debris on the riverbed. He drowned. As I listened to my father I pictured my little brother's pale and slender body being spotted by a stranger walking along the riverside. My brother being fished from the river by hooks and poles, careening and bumping into the bank, his head stroked by weed tresses. My brother in a mortuary. The water in his lungs being sampled, spores and a sodden blade of grass. My brother catalogued by a registrar and reduced to a number. Just another file. Ex-life.

My father told me a coroner's report was pending. He also asked if I would speak to Elizabeth. When she came on the phone it sounded as though she was panting, like a parched and exhausted dog. Her voice rasped and scraped like the cough my mother had had before the end. Elizabeth cried out that she felt responsible for what had happened, that she should have been with him. I mouthed some inane reassurances. I said I would come home straight away. Candidly, I felt relieved when I was able to get off the phone. I stood there for a moment, staring at a hotel lobby painting of red-jacketed huntsmen leaping over a hedge, their horses sleek and muscular.

I broke down in front of George. He was just as affected as I was and for more than an hour he cried over the loss of my brother. We sat in the hotel bar, while the manager tried to offer us the use of a private lounge so that we would not upset the other paying guests.

I never saw my room at the hotel. Instead, I said goodbye to George and walked back across the road. He wanted to come with me but I told him I needed to be alone. He was still in tears when I left.

I walked into the cool concourse of the station. The quietness came as a relief. I sat on a bench and watched a train glide in, the sound of its engine decreasing along a scale. Passengers got off and went about their business. The intricate, indifferent world just carried on. New people climbed aboard and the train eased away.

I stood up and walked, finding myself at the end of the platform, staring at the web of tracks. The loneliness of the outer edge of the station at the end of the day brought fear, the sense that I would be unable to deal with what lay ahead of me at home. I turned around, walked out of the station, headed away from the hotel and kept walking until I found a pub that did bed and breakfast. I drank for the rest of the evening, falling headlong and fully dressed into bed sometime after midnight.

I spent a further two days away. It just felt right. I could no more face home than I could face charging into battle. I made no contact with George who, I assumed, had left Norwich after one night at the hotel, as planned.

During my two days alone I found I had a heightened receptivity to the landscape. The sound of rain drumming through leaves in a forest, less percussive than melodic. The coolness of a raindrop on the back of the neck. I did not wear my watch and the minutes and hours folded into one another. My abandonment of my family in their time of need was, no doubt, terrible, but I had a strong, gut feeling that what I was doing was necessary for my sanity. I experienced my behaviour as an imperative. However, I can see now how selfish I was and am amazed that I could not see it then.

Eventually, I decided to go home without any more delay but I was running out of money. I hitched a ride from a lorry driver to the outskirts of South London and caught a local train from Croydon to Victoria, where the fear returned as the light started to fade at the end of another day. Beggars peered at me like interrogators. Their requests for money, whispered and growled through beards and hoods were like sneers, as though they were malevolent monks possessed of some salacious knowledge, leering through their cowls. Their words came from doorways and out of the shadows: 'Sorry to bother you, Sir.' I turned away again, caught the train back to Croydon and walked to a nearby mail depot. I found a van driver who was willing to give me a lift. He took me to a main road, from which I hitched another lift in a lorry around the M25, over the Dartford Crossing and into Kent.

I knew I was near the spot where Jack died. I asked the lorry driver to drop me off and made my way across ploughed fields and through a new housing development to a stretch of the river, the river which had simply wiped out Jack's life, leaving him to rotate in the water like a starfish twirling in its own, small orbit. Jack was gone, irrevocably, gone as completely as if he had never been born in the first place. No children, no adulthood, no women; barely an existence at all. The family obituaries would claim he had brought joy to all who had known him but in fact he, through his death, chiselled deep cuts of grief into all of us. Jack's pain radiated centrifugally from his corpse spinning slowly in the water. The black river ground on.

I headed back towards civilisation, gauging my path by the lights in the houses. I came to a street lit road. A cloud of breath purled over my shoulder. Not my breath. I halted.

'Gon-Gonzago,' said the voice.

'No.' My voice came out as a whisper.

'Gonzago. You did that, Victor. You did. I'm going to tell.'

I felt teeth latch onto the back of my neck. A lover's bite.

I span around, my arms flailing and thrashing, a whirling dervish of limbs. I toppled over and looked up at an open sky, at a last wraith of breath slithering into space. I heard the sound of footsteps running away and a short giggle.

It was close to midnight when I got home. The downstairs lights were still on. I turned the key, hearing its familiar click. I had made up my mind not to discuss Gonzago with my family. They had enough to worry them already and, in any case, I could not trust my own senses.

I stepped inside and was smothered by the warmth of the central heating. The lounge door opened and I saw my father come towards me. The flesh on his face was furrowed and his eyes were buried deep in their sockets. Bags hung below his eyes. I knew the same suffering was etched in my face, too. It was clear I had got it wrong about my own health and recovery, given what had happened to me as I had walked back from the river, but that would have to wait. For now, I was a mourning brother.

'Where have you been, Victor?'

'I'm sorry.'

'We were so worried.'

'I'm…'

'But the funeral. But, Jack. Where…?' He raised his hand to his brows.

They had been so worried about me that they had seriously thought about reporting me as a missing person to the police. George had been unable to help, as he had thought I was heading straight home when he said goodbye to me. He had told my father everything he knew. He was as mystified as the rest of them.

I could sense my father was trying to restrain his anger at me. He placed a hand on my shoulder as he spoke, yet his gaze kept flicking up to the ceiling. He breathed deeply. I looked down at my shoes and hummed in my head to keep his words at bay.

His took his hand away and reached down to a small table. He picked up a newspaper and pressed it against my chest. 'Read this,' he said.

It was the local newspaper. Jack's death was the front-page story. 'Selfish,' muttered my father as he walked back towards the lounge, 'fucking selfishness.' I had never heard him swear before. As he shut the door behind him I could see his fingers were trembling.

I scanned my eyes down the article. Katarina's name was mentioned several times. The newspaper stressed she was close to the spot where Jack had drowned and it was baffling that she would not have heard him shouting for help. It was all too obvious where they were laying the blame.

The article continued onto an inside page. Misadventure seemed the likeliest cause. There were reportedly no marks on Jack's legs to suggest he had become entangled in weeds, but there were some bruises on his torso, the cause of which was not known. There were no witnesses; a woman walking her dog had seen the young boy floating face down and had raised the alarm. The newspaper report added that Jack could not have been any great distance from the bank, given the fairly modest breadth of the river. Therefore, as he was considered to be a competent swimmer, allowing for his age and his slight build, it was not entirely clear what had happened. There was even a brief interview with Katarina, who admitted to reading a book while sitting on the riverbank, allowing Jack to escape from her view if not from her earshot. She also said she might have dozed off for a moment, explaining why she had not heard anything, but this only added to the newspaper's indignation, allowing it to suggest neglect.

The newspaper had taken a photograph of her, half-smiling, her hair trailing down over one half of her face. I had not seen her before. She was a pretty girl; shy, sympathetic. I looked away hurriedly. I did not understand how the newspaper could condemn without knowing the full facts.

My father stormed back into the hall before I could turn to the final paragraph. He snatched the paper from me and flung it to the ground. The sheets billowed out behind him. He stood right in front of me, breathing loudly. I could feel his hot, sour breath.

'How could you do this to us? You selfish, selfish bastard.'

'I'm sorry, I'm sorry. It was my way of dealing with it. I couldn't face being here. You could have delayed his funeral if you had wanted to.'

'You couldn't face being here. And us? Did we have the choice? Could we deal with it by running away? "Delay the funeral." Yes, let him lie on a cold slab like a piece of meat like any dead animal.' He paused. 'The poor boy. At least he's with his, with his mother now. And you, you're no better than that...slut!' He spat the word out.

'Who are you talking about?'

'I don't want her near this house again. Never. Never.' He continued to say the word as he pushed past me and up the stairs. I heard him walk into his bedroom and slam the door shut behind him. The word 'never' still hung in the air, while 'slut' rang in my head. My father never spoke like that. I looked ahead of me, too stunned to say anything, and saw Elizabeth's face peering at me around the lounge door.

She seemed older and the half-rimmed glasses she wore made her look like a schoolteacher. She placed her head on my shoulder and wept: 'My Jack's dead, my Jack's dead.' She said it quietly, as though it was a secret. Her hair grated against my cheek.

The first night was terrible. I lay in the comfort and familiarity of my own room, but throughout the night pictures of Jack flashed through my head. I also thought of the au pair I had never met. My father had stayed upstairs and it was Elizabeth who told me what had happened. My father had blamed Katarina for Jack's death and had thrown her out.

I kept thinking of the poor girl as I lay alone in my room. She was banished from her new home. She was being made to pay for the random and futile loss of a young life. I felt for her and instinctively wanted to offer her some comfort. I thought I could smell her perfume in the air. The photo in the newspaper lingered in my head.

The next morning Elizabeth told me she had spoken on the phone to Katarina, who was going to leave England and return to Czechoslovakia that same day, late in the afternoon. She was travelling down to Dover to catch the ferry back to the European mainland. I had thought of something I could do to make her feel better but wanted to keep it to myself. I asked Elizabeth if I could see her.

Before that came the visit to Jack's grave. They had buried him with my mother. We drove in silence, entering the cemetery through the high iron gates. We drove down a thin lane, surrounded by impeccably manicured lawns dotted with headstones. Magpies flitted and scavenged over the dead.

I brushed my hand over a furze of moss on a white headstone and saw a teddy bear on its back on a grave. We walked over to a freshly dug mound. The soil swelled pregnantly above the turf as if it was proud of its achievement. The gold writing on the black marble headstone described Melissa Harrow as a 'Devoted wife and mother.' Some of the paint had begun to flake away. Fresh wreaths were layered on top of the soil. Some of the leaves were already starting to rot and petals cartwheeled in the breeze. I felt strangely calm, looking beyond the grave to the rich, pristine grass.

Nothing was said, the headstone solid as a wall between us. After a few minutes we filed back to the car. I walked ahead of my father and Elizabeth. Someone sniffed behind me.

We drove home, again in silence, and drank weak coffee in the kitchen. I was pleased when my father left the house for a walk by himself. It meant we could visit Katarina without having to explain ourselves.

Elizabeth came with me as we drove in my father's car to an unkempt suburb and a street of rundown houses broken up into flats and bedsits. We found the place we were looking for. Katarina was sharing a bed-sit with another Eastern European girl and sleeping on the floor.

Katarina looked to me like a traumatised young woman. Her long, lank hair trailed along her shoulders. Her pale face looked down and to the side. I thought I might have seen her before but could not be sure; there was something familiar about the darkness that possessed her. She sat on the floor, her left leg stretched out along the carpet and her right leg bent at the knee and held in front of her, her hands wrapped round it, the fingers interlocking in front of her shin. She wore trainers, black canvas trousers and a white, Aran jumper. She kept saying 'I feel so responsible.' She pronounced it 'ris-pon-si-ble,' placing all of the emphasis on a shrill third syllable. She kept crying.

The police had interviewed her on the day of the accident and a zealous officer had arrested her on suspicion of being an illegal immigrant. Elizabeth had brought her passport to the station and Katrina had been released, but she wept as she described what had happened to her, how she had been locked up in a cell.

While she sat there on the floor of the bed-sit I felt I could sweep up all her guilt and heap it on myself. I felt strangely responsible, both for this pale girl sobbing on a threadbare carpet in a cold room and for Jack, face down, his body tugged seaward slowly. To hook him by the neck out of the water and into the judicial system and the administration of death seemed no less miserable and futile than the loss of his life in the river. I thought of his body inching and spiralling, nudged by the tide, ripped out of the water by a hook at the end of a pole.

I offered to drive Katarina to Dover. She said no but I kept asking until she said yes. Elizabeth had a doctor's appointment in town and said she would make her own way home. I had found out from Elizabeth, while we were driving over, that Katarina maintained no contact with what remained of her family and that she would try staying with some casual acquaintances in Prague until she could get a job and somewhere permanent to live. She was worried about what she would have to do to earn money. We left; all Katarina had in the world was one shoulder bag, though I found out how heavy it was as I carried it down the stairs.

Katarina thanked me repeatedly as we drove down to Dover. She also talked about her love for Jack. She broke down several times. 'It's like the devil has come into my life,' she said. I shuddered, recognising the sensation. She told me about being fingerprinted by the police. She cried again. She leant forward, the seat belt straining and creaking, her hair falling around her face. I thought about the police touching her hands, their large fists encircling her slender fingers, the sweat of their palms greasing her knuckles and nails. I thought of her fingerprints, slender matryoshka lines. I felt a whisper beginning to form, a guttural sound at the back of a throat. A voice that only I could hear: 'It was her, you know.' I shook my head. 'You know,' the voice told me again.

A car pulled past me in the outside lane, its engine revving angrily. I glanced to the right. It was a family group in an estate car. The chubby hand of a small child waved indiscriminately from the side window and then from the rear. The car pulled ahead and the figure of the child receded into a blur. I was oddly transfixed by the sight of a happy, family group. I felt the urge to confide in someone, to tell Katarina everything, but repressed the impulse. It would do me no good. My story would not be believed. I stared at the road ahead. The whisper in my throat gurgled up again. 'It was her, you know,' became 'You know' and then, 'No.'

Katarina and I swallowed up the miles of motorway until we began the long descent into Dover. I looked over at the sea as we drove down the hill. It was deathly still, sunk down below us.

There was a roundabout at the foot of the hill and we turned into the port, an intricate web of traffic lanes and berths for ferries and cruise ships. We parked up and walked in through automatic doors that seemed to shut behind us hurriedly, sealing us inside. I went to the toilet while Katarina bought her ticket. An idea I had had earlier came back to me. I was thinking about what the newspaper had said. It was understandably tempting to take the reactionary view, to lay blame on someone who, having only a tentative status in the country, could be branded wicked by a system eager to shed all responsibility, a system reluctant to acknowledge that the loss of a life can be purely meaningless. I understood precisely the need to project the blame elsewhere.

I returned to the booking hall and said goodbye, holding Katarina's hand for a few seconds before drawing her towards me and hugging her briefly. Her hand was cool to the touch; her hair smooth against the side of my face. She stepped away and I watched her float upwards on an escalator heading for the departure lounge.

Something was not right. I bounded up the escalator and tapped her on the shoulder. She turned around and smiled. We stood there, rising into the air in silence. At the top I said

I needed to talk to her and steered her back down a flight of stairs, my right hand placed firmly on her left elbow.

'What is wrong?' she asked.

'I've had a thought.'

I drove a stunned Katarina out of the port in my father's car and headed along the seafront. It was incredibly quiet. The pebbled beach was deserted. I pulled the car over to the side of the road and switched off the engine. I turned to her and let it all flood out. I told her everything. I told her all about Gonzago. She did not understand, shaking her head as I spoke. She grabbed her bag and clambered out of the car but I followed her and caught her. She looked into my face, frightened, but I did not want to debate anything.

I led her along the high harbour wall overlooking deep water. She tried to stand at a distance from me, looking down at the ground, but I would not let her stray too far, grabbing her sleeve and pulling her back towards me. No one else was in sight.

It was dusk. A disused hovercraft lay rusting on a broad concrete ramp, beneath us and over to our right. It was skeletal; curves of iron poked through black plastic sheeting blowing upwards in the wind. The hovercraft lay there, a dead and useless thing. Scavenging seagulls squatted on its roof. I saw one of them take a shit on it; a thick, white and ugly splurge. Rage clenched me, targeted against the machine for its own uselessness, its inability to fight against its fate, just a redundant hulk waiting to be scrapped. I seized up, every muscle tightened and I held my breath, but the feeling subsided and I relaxed, peering into the opaque and oil-skinned English Channel. I calmed myself down through deep breathing. Once recovered, I smiled at my own silliness. It had been a moment of irrationality, born of the grief I was trying to re-press. It was really nothing to worry about. I was calm, collected and rational, and soon Katarina disappeared from my view. I waved a friendly salute. Gone.

I thought of Jack again, drifting away, and at last I could cry like a mourning brother. It was a good release, a private letting go.

I needed to take a break on the journey home. I ate dinner alone at a roadside restaurant, washing the sweat from my hands and face in the toilet after placing my order. There was a lot of dirt under my fingernails. I dug it out and held my hands under the drier for a long time, lulled by the sound. My meal was waiting for me when I got back. The steak was rare, the mushrooms good. I complimented the food when the waitress came to take my plate. 'We always do our best, you know,' she said. I knew.

I know there's someone in my house. I sense her presence. I'm trying to say out loud, 'There's someone here. A woman,' but the words won't come out. I can't breathe.

I know I displaced a lot of my feelings about Jack's death, projecting them onto the figure of Katarina gliding away from me at Dover. Maybe my pursuit of her, the sprint up the escalator and the hand reaching for her shoulder, was compensatory. I was trying to pull back something that had been lost irrevocably. The subsequent rage and confusion that came over me when I stood with Katarina was also almost certainly linked to Jack. I felt a sense of futility about what had happened. It made no sense to deny the truth. It would be better to face it, to confirm it, to know the truth so it would no longer hold any fears for me. Through Katarina I tried, albeit imperfectly, to face it.

I had also been struck by Katarina's resemblance to Elizabeth. Both of them exuded an inconsolable sense of loss over my brother's death. I needed to do something with their grief, but whether my compulsion was to share it or to obliterate it, I honestly do not know. Katarina reminded me of someone else, too, but I could not pin that thought down. I behaved very badly towards Katarina. I accept that. However, I too had suffered a loss and it unquestionably affected my conduct.

None of us ever heard from Katarina again after that late afternoon in Dover, but I was unable to shake off a sense of responsibility for her. In fact, I often wondered about her. I regretted the fact that I had not dealt directly with my father's anger towards her. Had I done so, she might have been taken back into the house. Furthermore, my guilt extended into a wider sense of self-blame concerning all the things that had happened: Elizabeth's illness, my mother's death, Jack's death, Katarina's dismissal and the clear evidence that I had serious mental health problems. I was becoming the common denominator in a series of calamities.

I had been absent for so long. I had never done anything to help my family. Furthermore, I avoided the company of my loved ones even though I was now alongside them. We were beginning to look like a cursed organism and part of me wanted to divorce my fate from theirs. In addition, my physical health began to decline again. I had no appetite and no interest in anything, least of all academic work. I found it hard to summon the effort to do even basic things like shower and shave. My father tried to persuade me to move on but it was hard.

If I was deeply affected by my little brother's death, it was nothing compared to the effect it had on Elizabeth. For her, it was as if Jack's death, following the death of our mother, had cast a pall over the whole of her life. Nothing, she said, would ever be the same for her again. It was odd, therefore, how she, like me, often vented her grief by talking about Katarina and the injustice she had suffered by being blamed for the fatal accident. Katarina became the sounding board for our feelings whenever we were together and our father was absent, and in that way Katarina stayed with us.

I did not tell Elizabeth what had passed between me and Katarina. It would be difficult to describe to someone else how two virtual strangers had found themselves in a close, even confessional situation. It was the sort of thing that could never happen again. However, the more Katarina was defended by Elizabeth, the more I heaped guilt on myself. Part of me still felt I needed to blame someone. Someone had to have responsibility for Jack's death, even it was me. I could not ever fully accept that my little brother's drowning was just a random event in a meaningless world.

Elizabeth became more tactile, clinging on to people out of fear that they might be taken from her. In particular, in the evenings, she often slipped in behind me on the sofa, wrapping her arms around me and clasping her hands in front of my stomach. I suppose it was part of the grieving process and I honestly tried to relax around her but found it was impossible. I could not switch off, even in our quietest moments. I could not give myself over to the comforts and consolations offered by people to each other in a time of crisis. Sometimes I could feel the voice trying to get through to me, gurgling in my throat or brewing whispers in my ears, an insistent 'G...G...G...' and I had to force it away, singing in my head to drown out the sound. Elizabeth held on to me and I felt I was being pinioned. The voice faded to a surly growl. Elizabeth was as needy as a baby.

My family told me that returning to Oxford would give me back my sense of purpose but, for me, Oxford was about sickness and, more specifically, about a period of mental illness which I had no wish to revisit. Furthermore, Oxford was where Gonzago had found me. The idea of finishing my thesis was still appealing but I could not think of Oxford without fear. Its spires, courtyards and stone walls were no longer havens but prisons.

The decision to return was made for me.

'You are going back,' said my father.

I opened my mouth to speak.

'It's not a discussion point,' he said. 'You are going. No "ifs," no "buts." It's decided. I'll drive you there.'

I was too lacklustre to get into a serious argument with him. I resigned myself to his decision and gained consolation in the knowledge that I would be placing distance between myself and my family at a time when we were dragging each other down. The fear of Oxford was there but I was drowning at home.

Two days later, after another sleepless night, my father drove me back. I dozed for the final part of the journey, waking outside my flat. My father said he did not want to come in. I muttered a brief goodbye and groped for my key in my trouser pocket. He drove away, accelerating.

Everything was as I had left it six weeks previously: rings from coffee mugs on top of my computer monitor, the open wardrobe with shirts and trousers hanging over the doors. The mess of my Oxford life lay all around me. The last time I was here I had been looking forward to my holiday. Now I fell onto my bed, not bothering to undress, and slipped into the deepest, most restful sleep I had known for a long time.

In the morning my shirt was damp and stained with dribble. I showered, shaved and changed my clothes. I made toast and drank coffee. I had opened the window as soon as I had got out of bed but still felt lethargic. I took my coat and wallet, made sure I had my keys and went out. I walked towards town, down a flight of iron steps at a bridge and along the riverbank.

The path was dusty. A long spell of dry weather had sucked all the moisture out of the surface. I reached the Isis Tavern around opening time, bought a beer and sat in the garden at the bench closest to the river's edge. I saw lines of rowers splayed across the river, finding their rhythm, cutting crisply through the water. Their bodies were synchronised, knees angling up towards their chests before thrusting down flat again. A rower from a crew of four glanced up at me as his craft arrowed by. He was young, powerful, his complexion ruddy, his mouth a perfect 'O' as he blew out. His breath gushed into the air, hauled up from the engine of his lungs. I looked back: silent, paler. I thought about his world. The sweat and camaraderie, the boisterous laughter, the easy joy in his own physicality.

I do not know how long I sat there. Eventually, without finishing the last of my flat beer, I walked home, switched the computer on and sat in front of it. I stared at the screen. A cauldron of words and numbers stirred within me but none of them would be drawn to the surface. I could barely move. The minutes lingered and the blank screen remained blank. I clicked on 'file,' 'exit,' and flicked off the monitor. I looked up at the phrenological head. The face returned my stare and its closed mouth twitched up slightly at the edge, as if in a smirk. It looked as if it might speak, as though its lips were about to part and a sound form at the back of its throat. I walked away before it could do anything else. I felt tired again by the late afternoon and had another full night's sleep.

I returned to the pub the next day and at the same time but saw no rowers. I was sitting at the same bench, wearing the same clothes, my hands cradling another flat beer. The air was still and silent, the weather humid. I finished my pint and returned to the bar. The inside of the pub, too, was deserted. A longhaired girl behind the bar served me without making eye contact. She placed my change noiselessly on the counter and turned away, out of sight. I looked around. The lights on the gambling machine winked at me.

I went back outside, sat in my place, took a large mouthful of my drink, and another. I looked around; it was unusual to be the only customer, even at this early hour. The silence and the stillness were overpowering, like waiting for an orchestra to commence its overture. The silence became heavier still, swelling in the heat. It rose up around me and I moved slowly like I was underwater.

I was not alone. I was being watched. There was a pair of eyes searching me out. I could not move a limb, unclench my jaw or even blink. I tried to force my right forearm to turn around but it was numb, lying there helplessly.

The eyes sought me out like searchlights hunting down an escaped prisoner. The sound of my own breathing battled with the silence and I felt as though I was heaving oxygen out of a compressed tank. The Earth was juddering down to an absolute halt in space. I sucked in a breath and stopped: all I could hear was my own heart beating. The river was deserted. The water surface static. Trees held their pose. The grass froze.

He was seated at the bench behind me, the 'G' sound forming at the back of his throat. Even though I could not see him I knew it, just as I knew he was reaching over to me, just as I knew that his hand was stretching out and his crooked finger, all veins, bones and nails, was going to jab me in the right shoulder blade. I wrenched my jawbone loose, gathered up all of my willpower and snapped 'Fuck off!' as I finally span around to face him.

He sat there, upright, with his elbows on the table and his hands clenched into fists. The muscles on his forearms stood proud. His brow was furrowed and his head was turned very slightly to one side, but whether his expression suggested curiosity, pain or contempt, I could not tell.

I spewed up a mouthful of bile down myself, stuttering 'Get away from me!' as I staggered back from the table, losing my balance, stumbling back onto the path, scrambling to the edge of the riverbank. I heard a click. The water started to flow again, waiting beneath me like a crocodile gliding towards its prey. It lapped against the bank like lips being licked.

He stood up, took a couple of steps towards me and paused. When he spoke he was calm, his voice low and quiet: 'I expected this. I frighten you. I know this is going to be hard for you, but try to listen to me.' He stepped forward and stood over me. The river heaved against the bank.

I stared. He was my size but he looked stronger than me. He reminded me of myself before my illness. I concentrated on his face and could see that he resembled me startlingly in every way, except he was calm while I was a twitching bundle of limbs on the floor, my legs shaking too much to bear my own weight as I tried and failed to stand. A bizarre sense of injustice seized me, an indignant feeling that this event had no right to happen.

'Come on,' I spat the words at him. 'I'll fucking kill you.' I scrambled to my haunches and sprang at him. He stepped away and I stumbled forward and sideways, toppling back into the pub garden before falling down, scraping my cheek against the edge of the bench. I fell face down onto cigarette butts, dry dirt and a patch of dead grass. I stopped for a second and thought about what had become of me. I had always prided myself on my self-control and my intellect. I had suppressed anger whenever I had felt its low growl rise within me. Now it was pouring out and I lacked the strength to stand in its way.

'Calm down,' he said, walking back towards me. 'I don't want to hurt you.'

'Look. Whatever this is about, it stops now. Now, right now.' I stood up again, climbing up against the bench for support. I turned around, breathed deeply, stepped forward and pressed my forehead against his.

He stood his ground. 'Will you not listen to me Victor? This is about you and me; no one else. I have nobody. I have been waiting for you to return to Oxford. If you will only listen you can do yourself and your loved ones a lot of good, or spare them harm at least.'

'Why are you doing this to me? You're some devil. Leave me alone, just leave me alone!' I broke down. My face slid down his and I fell to my knees, my forehead resting against his belt.

'It won't hurt you to listen to me, Victor.' He sighed like a mildly exasperated parent. He was close, his breath bathing my face with its stale warmth. I looked up. He smiled and I wanted to break my glass in his face.

I hauled myself upright and stared at the path heading back into town. I could run but the dust would be like sand, sapping my energy. It was no use. He would easily catch me. I sat back down, opposite him.

Silence.

'Tell me a bit more about what Gonzago looks like, Victor.'

'He looks like me, Doctor.'

'Does that suggest anything to you?'

'He is real, you know.'

'What did he say, Victor?'

Silence.

'Victor, I'd like to talk to Gonzago. I'd like to hear what he has to say.'

I sensed a breakthrough.

Silence.

'It's OK, Victor. Let him speak. Let him have a voice. It will help. We'll try hypnotherapy again.'

The sound of stifled sobbing.

Dr Field

I suggested we stop for the day. Harrow agreed. He asked if we could start early the next day.

I could not help noticing that despite what we were discussing as the day had progressed, he seemed to be enjoying himself much of the time. He immersed himself fully in the fantasy and became more expansive, modulating his voice for different characters. It is an encouraging sign, partly because he is not falling back on his standard defences and partly because it suggests he will be responsive to hypnotherapy, if I try my five session approach.

I had noticed, too, how Harrow's body posture had become upright the further he went into his story. He only slumped when Gonzago appeared in person. The second visual hallucination was much more sustained than the first but essentially Harrow was still seeing himself, though he did not seem to recognise the fact. My expectation is that the hallucination will have coincided with a high level of activity in the visual cortex, but there is no way of proving it.

Aside from the hallucinations, which I intended to probe further, I was concerned by Harrow's lack of grieving. He had repeated with his brother's death what he had done or, more accurately, not done with his mother's. To Harrow's credit he recognised the oddity and unacceptability of his own behaviour in shunning his family after Jack's death although, from my professional point of view, I can recognise the lack of an emotional response as a schizophrenic symptom. The one, acknowledged outpouring of grief was the odd incident with the family's au pair. Even here, however, it was a relocation. The feelings about his mother and brother were vented elsewhere onto a peripheral figure who had been expelled from the family unit. It was like a scolded child releasing anger on a doll, clubbing its head or pulling its limbs off. Not that Harrow did any of those things, I think. A moment of strong, irrational feeling was deflected onto a young woman who disappeared from his story.

Maybe none of it happened. Harrow's calm relaying of the story was certainly odd. He seems to need to detach from or even expel the feminine in all aspects of his life. Perhaps that is a core aspect of his criminality and disease.

If his story is true, at least in part, I wonder what happened to the young girl. Did she make it home? Surely she did. She just went her own way. I thought about Jack, too. Death by drowning must be awful. The desperation. I tried not to think too much about it. It was too close to home.

It was clear to me that all Harrow's repressed, pent-up energy would not be satisfied fully by sublimation. It would have to be discharged somehow, at its original source. The repressed returns. I know.

I decided, when my turn came, to start Harrow off by giving the simplest algorithm of grief I knew: tears, silence, song. You have to start the healing with tears; the smallest child knows that. In the meantime, hypnotherapy was, in my view, the best means of accelerating his treatment, deepening his immersion and, hopefully, exposing his trauma.

Harrow called out 'Bye' as I left the room.

I tried to read an article in bed last night but could not concentrate. Opening that bottle of wine was not a good idea. But I needed to slow down. I needed to block out a line of thought that was tormenting me.

I should have stopped after the first glass. The empty bottle lay on its side this morning, the top of the bottle like an incriminating eye.

Something else: Harrow talked about the phone call when he was told his brother had died. Elizabeth came on the phone and her voice reminded Harrow of his mother. He clearly connects the two of them, more closely than he is prepared to acknowledge. That may prove to be significant.

I revisited the house where I grew up, directly after Margaret's funeral. It belonged to strangers. I just looked on from

the outside. Blank walls; locked doors. I pictured rooms
choked with dust motes, the skin of the dead.

A dream of a woman gasping for air. She was not in water, she was lying on a mattress in a dark room but she could not breathe, thrashing like a fish plucked from the water. I could not see her face.

Staring at a house with drawn curtains. I know she's there. She knows I'm outside.

A girl with her friends. She knew me. I knew her, too, but didn't know why. She was too young to be my contemporary. Maybe she was a work colleague at some time, or a student.

   We're talking. Her friends are laughing. One of them has his hand close to my holdall. I draw it closer to me. More laughter. Are they having fun or feeling awkward, or do they feel at risk from me?

Hypnotherapy – session #1

'Victor, can you see the small handle on the drawer up in the top corner of the room. The gold handle?'

'Yes.'

'I want you to concentrate on that handle, on its small shape and bright colour. Breathe deeply while I count down from ten. When I have finished I will ask you to close your eyes.'

I count down. Slow, getting slower.

I drop my voice. 'Close your eyes.' They shut, slowly.

'Gonzago? Would you like to talk? Tell me anything. What's the first thing you remember?'

An intake of breath. A quiet voice. Like Harrow's, only more hesitant, a voice finding itself.

'I remember walking into a room of older children. They were probably only nine or ten years old but they looked like giants. They formed a circle around me. I was peering out for someone.

'As a small child, I used to close my eyes and swear I was having visions. I always saw terrible things; an ancient battle with children being speared and gutted, or a suited gunman breaking into homes and shooting whole families.

'I was in a care home, a lost property depot for the bad children who would never be collected by anyone. I ran away when I was fifteen. I broke into the office with another boy, looking for keys to the main doors. We opened the filing cabinet and read all about ourselves. I saw a report on me. I can't remember what it said. I grabbed the keys and ran for my life. As I left the room I saw my compatriot was pissing on the open files. I never saw him again. I assume he was caught.

'I unlocked the main door and ran.'

Silence.

'Then what happened, Gonzago?'

'I was living with two others in a shelter in a forest. We had found some sheets of corrugated iron. We propped them up against each other, secured them at the base with rocks and stones and covered the hut with branches. We lined the floor with tarpaulin.

'It was getting cold, late autumn, and I lay huddling by a fading fire outside the hut, watching the embers. I fell asleep, rolled over and into the red hot ashes. Heat seared through me, wringing my spine, hammering into my head. I screamed, waking the others. They flung themselves on me, bellowing. I passed out.

'For three days after the burning I lapsed in and out of consciousness. The others brought me water which I threw up. After those three days I could stand up and walk once more but it was a long time before I was back to normal. I felt raw. Sometimes the pain made me double up. The burnt skin peeled away in shavings and scrolls. I felt like I was starting out again with a freshly made body. The new skin grew, tracing its web across my flesh, cell linking to cell.

'I moved to a squat in South London. It was cold, dark and dangerous. Damp blossomed on the walls. Floorboards had been ripped up and thrown onto a fire. Rats and mice ruled the house at night-time. I had a badly swollen finger from a bite I had received as I slept. Most of the others used drugs.

'A young runaway staying there was on the game. She had been arrested the previous day. The police had held her for twenty-three hours. When they let her out her whole nervous system was screeching for the next hit. Back at the squat she spiked up and switched off. I saw the light in her eyes go out; clear, bright blue irises glazing over and misting. She sat there, the point of the needle still lodged in her upturned forearm, making a small, bulbous lump in her flesh. The inside of her arm was riddled with livid, red dots. Her jaw hung slack and a thin stream of watery dribble ran from her lower lip onto the bare floor. I stared into her nothing of a face and saw the future. The moment was almost biblical. I walked out of the squat and never walked back.'

Silence. Harrow's eyelids flutter. His breathing quickens. He is coming out of the trance.

'Ok, Victor. I'm going to count from one up to ten. When I get to ten you will wake up.'

The count back. The room seems to soften. His eyes open. He looks afraid. I tell him we will take a break.

I was surprised at how quickly he had gone under and how deeply. I want to move fast, but not too fast.

I went to my office to make a couple of notes.

Harrow

I have made compromises. Plenty of them. They have medicated me half to death to try to silence me. But one thing on which I will not compromise is Gonzago. If I had accepted what they wanted me to believe about him my life would have been less tough, but the truth matters. The truth will set you free but it is difficult, so difficult.

This doctor, Field, at least listens. He can help me. Maybe he could get me out of here. His methods are unusual. No one has ever hypnotised me before. When I woke up I could not remember much of what I had said.

I glance at Dr Field sometimes. When he is concentrating his body language changes. He hunkers down, making himself small. I do not know whether he is timid or preparing himself for launch like a cannonball. He is planning something, but if he thinks he is impervious he is wrong. He is changing. Sometimes when I look at him he is imperious in his chair. Other times he looks like a frightened little boy. He has a story, too. He needs to tell it. The repressed returns. He has to start his own healing, release his own grief.

I am getting sudden headaches, and numbness, too. It is probably my medication.

Dr Field

Schedule

1. Write up first draft of article in three months.

2. Aim for a journal paper instead of a conference presentation. Need to get this into print straight away. Need to get it known as mine. Others may be working in the same field. My ideas have been stolen before. First to market is everything. Second is nowhere.

3. I will need to build support. Could try UK Council for Psychotherapy. Build a coalition of the willing. Have no inroads to the General Medical Council at the moment. Press coverage would be useful but that is down to luck. Maybe I could write letters to journalists or to MPs. Need to be more strategic in my thinking.

Some odd parallels are coming out. Things Harrow says. Must keep it at bay. Therapy is not a one way broadcast. I need to be on my guard. It is time for self-discipline.

One of the nurses tried to start a conversation with me this morning. Told me her parents were first cousins. Said her father was violent, too, and that he is dead and her mother is in a home. I have no idea why someone would be happy to make that sort of thing public knowledge. When you give away information you put yourself in danger. Therapy is safer. It is a walled garden, though you are not alone in there. Talking in public is a different matter.

That's how my father ended up; in a home. I didn't visit.

Googled Maggie. Nothing there, nothing I had not seen before anyway. One photo, looking straight to camera. Nothing in the background.

As Gonzago, Harrow sets up a stage on which repressed aspects of himself can perform. There are, however, common denominators. His scenarios: the care home, the runaway and the squatter, contain vulnerable figures, all on society's margins. It is consistent with the withdrawal and suspicion typical of schizophrenia. His fellow escapee in the care home is more animalistic, a repressed aspect of Harrow which, predictably, he left behind.

Why, when he was voicing the fantasy about living in the forest, did Harrow have two companions? In reality he has two siblings, but there is no parental figure in his fantasies, just the institutional coldness of a care home, suggestive of his cold father, or perhaps of his own incarceration after his prosecution. The care home may also be related to the pain of losing his mother. It is all too much so he locks it away and lives an emotionally frigid existence, possibly underlined when, in the fantasy, he has nothing to say about his own case file. Harrow is not known to himself, but the same is true for many people. I know a thing or two about coldness as a defence. It is one of the reasons why I have stayed single.

I am also interested in the fire episode. It is the opposite of coldness, a narrative of self-immolation. It seems to me that in this instance Harrow is replaying his sickness in Oxford after the first visual hallucination and the botched suicide attempt. His story is about three days of sickness, of lapsing in and out of consciousness. Alternatively, the experience in Oxford may have been a delayed reaction to his mother's death, an eruption of grief he had tried to repress.

Similarly, the fantasy of the drug addict replays the vivid nightmare he had about his mother during his first psychotic episode. Furthermore, he focused on the girl's arm, just as he had focused on his mother's arm when he saw her for the last time. He relocates his attention away from the centre of his trauma. He cannot face the centre: not yet.

In the fantasy the girl is a sex worker as well as an addict. I do not know what to make of that at the moment. He may be projecting bad feelings onto his mother. Maybe he is unconsciously angry at her for dying, for abandoning him.

I also asked him about the first thing he remembered. The approach is taken from the Gestalt school of psychology, which regards first memories as a type of codex, a pattern, an organising and explanatory image for a life. Harrow, as Gonzago, described an experience characterised by suspicion, isolation and fear. He views the world as a threat. He may be right.

Finally, I was taken by the structure of his words as Gonzago. He talks in snippets and vignettes, just as he did when we started therapy. Perhaps he will open up again. He needs to.

A dream of a body in the boot of a car. Maybe dead, maybe not.

Hypnotherapy – session #2

'Victor, we're going to do the same again. Concentrate on the gold handle and breathe deeply as I count down. Ten... nine...eight...seven, eyes getting heavy...six...five...four... Three, eyes closing. Two...one. Eyes closed.

'Talk to me, Gonzago.'

'There was a girl, Anna. A girl with ripped jeans, a pierced eyebrow and nose and long dreadlocks. A good dancer. She had had training. Did not speak to her family. Did not like talking. She liked dancing. She did it properly. She could spin, crane and arch back. She could make herself tiny. She could look like she was levitating when she moved.

'I used to watch her through a crack in the door, focusing on the tightness of the ribbons on her pointe shoes. I lifted them up once when she was out. They weighed so little, offering no cushioning, barely encasing her soft feet. It was like handling a baby's slippers.

'I wondered what would happen to Anna as she aged, as the limbs lost their natural grace. She could easily be staring at fifty years of loss as she dropped from her heights, as she lost her absolute freedom of movement. It is better that things like that do not happen. A dancer who cannot dance is nothing, like a painter who cannot paint is nothing, like a thinker with Alzheimer's. An early death is better.'

Silence. I felt this train of thought was going nowhere. Just grudges. Just reactionary thoughts. Harrow needed a prompt.

'Who else did you know, Gonzago? Who else did you know?'

'There was a blind man, Mr Lacy. He needed a helper and live-in companion. His two, grown up children had flown the nest.

'I did a bit of everything for Mr Lacy. I drained his radiators when the central heating would not work. I trimmed the hedge. I cooked.

'I spent the winter sheltered from the hail and rain. Looking from my window, I could see the reflections of the lights in the puddles in the street below, yet know that I was going to go to sleep in the cosy, single room, pulling my duvet tight across my body for the sheer sense of warmth and comfort.

'Sometimes I stood in my room, stroking the vinyl wallpaper or hooking my fingers through the holes in the net curtains. That was all it took to make me happy.

'Mr Lacy liked to take walks. I adored my life, cosseted in the smiles that strangers would give me when they saw me take the arm of an old, blind man. His fingers held on to me tightly.

'Mr Lacy told me about his daughter, Diane, who lived in Seattle with her American partner. I could picture her and I could also picture myself with her, my arm around her waist or wrapped reassuringly around her shoulder, the two of us standing in front of a picket-fenced suburban home with a happy labrador or setter gambolling around our feet and maybe a baby on the way. Vacations in a large camper van, touring across places with wide, open names, like Wyoming. I pictured prairies and mountains, all under an enormous sky. I airbrushed her partner out of the fantasy. Mr Lacy told me too about his son, Tony, who worked for a charity in Ghana. I was pleased Tony was far away.'

Dr Field

Harrow jolted. I asked him if he was OK. He did not respond. I brought him back out of the trance.

It is frustrating. I have to look after him, but despite the randomness of his stories I am sure he is on the fringe of releasing. I am certain of it. He is flitting from story to story, but if he stays on one he may go deeper and expose the trauma. I need to check his medication. His most recent file note shows he complained of a sudden headache.

Harrow inhabits the role, enacting a play within a play. It is enlightening to see this side of him. For someone who is generally ill at ease he enters into a kind of flow state as Gonzago. He is much more restless as himself. He self-identifies as Harrow, but is he more complete and less fractured as Gonzago? It is like watching the ego emerge from behind the super-ego. The cold ascetic is replaced by a creature with fears and drives.

Gonzago allows Harrow to articulate the aspects of himself he normally represses. I see different facets of his character but some motifs reappear time after time: vulnerability, or marginal status. The only partial exception was the dancer, who seemed to represent a different feature of his repression. At the time I felt it was going nowhere but now I see I was wrong because the story expresses his feelings about his adopted sister. It was interesting that she was separated from her family in the fantasy, released from an inhibiting context, or it might express her being an adoptee. More interesting still was the voyeurism, which is clearly indicative of repressed desire for her on Harrow's part.

I had a sister, too.

Harrow's fantasies are increasingly elaborate. Not only does he project into a relationship with a blind man, he projects further, hypothesising a relationship with one of the blind man's children. It is like placing two mirrors against each other. You get an endless series of images, all distracting from the core object. His defence mechanisms are highly complex. He gives the blind man, a father figure, two children, but Harrow places them far away in different continents. Harrow had two siblings; both are now dead. Harrow, through Gonzago, posits a relationship with one of them, another indicator of repressed desire for his own sister.

Harrow's case could go far. I may need a media coach if I end up doing interviews. I am jittery by nature. I lean forward too much, like I am curling up. I cannot do that in front of the cameras.

I was thinking recently about the kind of people who make good psychotherapists. They have to be able to detach, to construct a perspective and a treatment programme. They also have to avoid being revolted by or enmeshed in what they hear. And what makes people able to detach? Some of it is from professional training but some of it is more formative. People who have had to practise detachment. We often have a lot more in common with our patients than we like to admit.

Reviewing the treatment thus far, it is interesting how Harrow intellectualises love. It is about analysis, not about feelings. He stands back and avoids immersion. Something happened to make him cauterise himself in this way. The death of Harrow's mother was quite late in formative terms. Either something preceded it or something happened later to amplify it, to bring it all flooding back and thus challenge his attempts at repression. That said, analysing love is like analysing humour. As soon as you start you neutralise it. Both states are about the experience.

I need Harrow to explore one of his fantasies in more detail. I missed an opportunity with Anna the dancer, but Lacy the blind man seems to be the one with the most potential, as it seems to me that the figure of Mr Lacy is going to allow him to explore his feelings about his father. The father he murdered.

A dead fox in an alleyway.

A dream of giving a lecture. I am fluent, evidential and assertive. Tough questions just bounce off me.

    The students file out. One of them leaves a piece of paper on a desk. There is handwriting on it.

    'This guy wants you to see what he's got. What a ho.'

Harrow

Dr Field projects professionalism but not empathy. He is sharp but lacks emotional intelligence. There is a missing part of him, a space that needs to be filled.

After the hypnotherapy session, as we both rearranged ourselves on our chairs, I asked him what books and music he liked. He was caught off guard and had to collect himself. He was keen to hear about my favourites but did not want to say anything about his own. It seems to me that he does not like me trespassing on his personality. He has built a wall around himself. I do not know why he has done that, but I do know from experience that walls are not impregnable. There are more things going on here than his professional practice.

I look around my room. The windows need cleaning.

Hypnotherapy – session #3

The countdown from ten to one.

'Tell me more about Mr Lacy, the blind man.'

'He received a cassette tape in the post one morning. It was from his son. He played it while I was in the kitchen cleaning up after breakfast. I heard it all. Tony's voice was soft, just like Mr Lacy's. Tony said he was in a loving relationship with a local girl and they were expecting a child. It seemed more likely they would settle in Ghana than return to England. He felt confident about being made headmaster of the school he was working in.

'After the tape finished and the "Play" button jumped up with a thud, I peeked into the room and saw tears pouring down Mr Lacy's silent face. It was like watching a mask cry. A shaft of sunlight spread out across the middle of the room but he sat in the shade. The silence reverberated with his son's words. The small, battery powered tape recorder slunk down on the floor in front of him. Mr Lacy suddenly looked very small and frail. An old man in a faded armchair, head

132

bowed, waiting for the end. He did not talk to me about the tape.'

Silence. I needed to press on.

'Can you tell me more about Mr Lacy?'

'He had come from a good, wealthy family. His father had been a financier and, when he died, Mr Lacy had taken over the company.

'Mr Lacy had invested heavily in overseas mining companies, along with a business partner. However, the speculations all floundered. His partner cut his own losses and left Mr Lacy to fend for himself. The company folded. Mr Lacy had enough money to provide for himself and an amount to leave to each of his children, but he had lost a lot. A long-standing weakness in his eyes accelerated, leading to his blindness.

'He began to trust me more and more. I made withdrawals from the bank on his behalf, first of all with him and later on my own while he stayed at home. The staff got to know my face, often giving me a cheerful wave when I arrived. I was the Good Samaritan.

'I found myself thinking about Mr Lacy's money and the difference it could make.'

Harrow swallowed a couple of times.

'I started to take a little money from Mr Lacy's account. It seems terrible now but at the time it did not appear to be such a big deal. It was only money. The amounts, individually, were trivial. But I know I should not have done it.

'It was easy. I regularly withdrew small sums to keep me going. I had learnt how to forge his signature. I knew everything about his accounts: balances, direct debits for bills, when his pension was paid. I bought clothes; I had decent ones for the first time in my life. I liked the feel of the notes in my hand, too. They gave me confidence.

'I knew it was only a matter of time before I was found out. I made a conscious decision to confess to Mr Lacy, trusting in the warmth that had grown between us. I believed that if I told him everything, told him I would repay every penny, he would understand and forgive. I decided to tell all but my courage kept failing me. I kept putting it off and meanwhile I kept stealing. The total amount grew, dripping from his accounts.

'Mr Lacy invested more and more of his trust in me, which made me feel even worse. I knew I would have to confess all to him and deal with the consequences.'

Harrow's posture shifted. He became more upright in the chair. His voice rose.

'One evening I decided to tell all, there and then.

'Mr Lacy sat in the old armchair in the lounge. His hands rested firmly on the antimacassars draped over the arms. I had washed them the previous day. They were ice-white and crisp.

'There were no lights on in the room. He was motionless, his features barely discernible in the darkness. He became aware that I was standing by the door.

'"Come in," he said, softly, turning his head to the left.

'"Can I speak to you for a few minutes?"

'"Of course, what is it?"'

Harrow's eyes flicked open but he was oblivious to my presence, temporarily blind. He started straight ahead. He was doing two voices. His own, as Gonzago, had become clear and more assertive. Mr Lacy's was soft and fragile, almost feminine.

'I sat down on the low sofa, facing Mr Lacy. I knew every second was precious, that if I hesitated I would lose my nerve, but I did not know where to start. His head moved again and I was staring into his face. The tired brown eyes shifted to the right, glazed over and focused on nowhere.

'"What's the matter?" Mr Lacy asked.

'"I have nobody. No family. No one. I see how you feel about your children and I know it's something really good."

'"Don't worry about that. You're young. Your life's just beginning, not like mine. You will have your own family."

'"I'm a good person, Mr Lacy, but I've done something bad, something that would make people, specifically you, hate me."

'"That's a pity, but can't you put it right?"

'"I'm going to try."

'"Good. Would you like to tell me what it is?"

'"I committed a crime."

'"What, when you were a boy? Don't worry about that. Everyone holds some deep secret. It's not a life or death matter, surely?"

'I felt a surge of relief, making my confession feel more like liberation than a burden. Mr Lacy was a good man, a kind man and a forgiving man. I knew it would be all right and he would let me make it up to him somehow.

'"Do you want to tell me what it is now?" His voice lilted over the question.

'A pause.

'"I've been stealing from you."

'"You've been…?"

'"Stealing. From you."

'"I don't…I don't…Stealing what? Money? How much?"

'"I don't know…Quite a lot."

'"Great God! Who are you? Who are you? Answer me!"

Lacy banged his fists on the arm of his chair. One of the antimacassars slid off and glided to the floor. A roar leapt from the base of his throat. His teeth were bared, yellow pegs dangling from pared-back gums. Spit splattered over his lower lip and down onto his chin.'

Harrow stood up from his chair. He was shaking. He started shouting.

'I flung myself at the old man. I dragged him from his throne and threw him to the ground. He squatted like a frightened animal. I jumped on him, spun him around on his back and pounded him with my fists, blow after blow straight down into his mouth. My weight kept him down on the floor as punch after punch drove down onto his eyes, nose and jaw. His useless eyeballs bounced around their sockets. His hands and legs waved and splayed like a beetle on its back.

'I grabbed his throat with both hands and squeezed, my thumbs overlapping across his Adam's apple, plunging into the hollow of his neck. I put all my strength into the grasp like I was wringing out a sodden towel. Bone and skin gave way. I heard a soft and drawn out crunch and a final sigh leaking from the mouth, sounding like relief. The heat of his last breath bathed my face and his mangled body relaxed, drained of life. I stood up, breathing heavily, feeling nothing.'

Harrow looked down; he was spent. He slumped back into the chair.

He spoke again. Gently, this time.

'My arms hung down by my sides. All I could hear was the sound of my own breathing. There was a stillness.

'Slowly, feeling started to seep back. A wish crystallised in my head as I stood over the dead, blind man. I wished I had never been born.

'I stepped back from him, leaving his body where it lay, walked out of the house and closed the front door behind me. I ran away into the darkness, keeping my head down and not looking back.

'I spent the night walking, not wanting to go back to the room where his frail body lay unwanted and twisted like an aborted foetus on the floor. The temperature fell and still I could not return, walking the streets of the suburbs, heading in towards the city.

'I saw lights in lounges, bathrooms and bedrooms of barrel-chested, semi-detached homes. Their comfortable lives just cruised on and on while mine had sunk and drowned. I would gladly have hurled explosives through their precious double-glazing, anything that would shatter their complacency and haul them down to my level.

'I walked past a park, climbed over the iron railings and headed across to the children's play area. A row of swings, mostly broken, lay suspended beneath a triangular, iron frame. I found one that still worked and sat down, rocking. All was lost. I put my feet down and grazed to a halt. I stood up and walked over to a small playhouse. It had a pointed roof and a large, heart-shaped window in the door. I bent down, climbed in and lay on the floor, curled up.

'It was still pitch black when I woke. The children's area was a safe enclave, an innocent space in a corrupt world. I went back over to the swing and fell asleep again, slumped in the seat with the iron chain pressed up against my face.

'I woke as the sun rose. My frozen fingers were wrapped tightly around the chain. A fine dust of rust flecks lay scattered across my hand. I started walking again, the damp clothes cloying at my skin. I itched and it was impossible not to scratch.

'I went back to the park and the swings in the afternoon. I rocked back and forth while a gaggle of scruffy, open-mouthed children stared at me. I returned their stares and one of them, a boy of about eight, spat on the ground in front of me.

'Hunger and tiredness had gripped me by late afternoon. Vivid recollections of a cat I had taken in at my London squat came back. A scrawny thing, black with a white bib. The day the cat failed to appear, never coming back. The vague sense of resentment I felt against it over the next few weeks. A glimpse of a strikingly similar cat in the long grass.

'I walked beyond the last boundary of the park, trying to keep a grip on my thoughts, and stumbled into dense woodland. I found a sheltered, secluded spot where I could lie down and sleep, falling out of the world for a couple of hours.

'It was dark again when I woke up. By now the cramping pains of hunger were too much to resist. I no longer had the strength to fight against the inevitable. I walked back to the street. I saw the house from some distance away. It was the only one in the row without any lights on. A lone streetlight shone down on the pavement.

'I let myself in and headed straight down the hall into the kitchen, not daring to look in the lounge or switching the lights on. I grabbed what cold food I could find in the fridge and wolfed it down. I made a cup of coffee and sat at the kitchen table, hunched in front of my drink, letting the steam bathe my face. I wrapped my hands around the cup and the heat scalded my skin.

'I stared at the plain, white door, solid as a coffin lid. I stood up, pushed it open and stepped into the dark room.

'He was on his back, his left arm trailing limply along his side. His right arm lay on his chest; it was bent at the elbow and at the wrist, with the gnarled hand underneath his chin. The room stank of his shit. But despite his appearance, with his weak and spindly legs bent at the knees and the stench catching in my nose and throat, I sensed a wisdom about him. Beaten and throttled out of life, he now knew something I did not know. I stared at him and pulled the folds of his sagging eyelids over his useless eyes. His skin was soft, moth-like.

'I sat there for a few more hours, raising his eyelids again with my thumb and staring at his bulging fish-eyes until daylight came. The eyes were empty and glazed like an old dog's.'

Silence.

I counted from one to ten. Harrow woke. He looked confused. We sat without saying anything for a couple of minutes. He told me he needed to be alone and poured himself a glass of water from his plastic jug. His hand shook. I left, found a nurse in the corridor and asked for Harrow to be kept under close observation for the rest of the day. She asked me if everything was OK. Maybe she heard the noise when Harrow was shouting, or maybe I looked different. Harrow had stunned me.

The old man's eyes were hemmed in like a baby kitten's. I said, 'It's OK. It's going to be OK.' His eyes opened. They bulged out. He could see. I called out, 'Maggie! Come quickly Maggie!' My own shouting woke me up.

A dream of the family cat from when I was a boy. The day it died. Its neck was broken, its head lolling forwards onto its chest. Wondering how it had happened.

Dr Field

The obvious analysis of the fantasy is that Lacy is Harrow's father and the Gonzago persona allows Harrow to play through his contradictory feelings in that regard, as well as dramatising the moment when he killed his father, and how he, Harrow, reacted. His file notes show he stabbed his father rather than strangled him but both deaths feature close, even intimate proximity.

Furthermore, Lacy inherited the family firm, just as Harrow's father did, and Lacy had an unreliable business partner, just like Harrow's father.

The blindness is a complicating factor. It may not be going too far to see the blindness as symbolic castration and thus, instead of the father being a powerful and authoritative figure, he is vulnerable, drained of his potency. While Harrow was speaking as Lacy his voice became almost feminine.

It is interesting to see Harrow exploiting the father figure's vulnerability when it was played through the figure of Gonzago. His previous fantasies constructed Harrow as the exploited, but in this fantasy he is the exploiter. There is the theme of betrayal, too. Gonzago betrayed Lacy by stealing from him. Harrow betrayed his family by absenting himself after Jack's death, missing the funeral. Harrow acknowledges his guilt in the fantasy.

The periphery is also interesting. The two children are swept away by being in different continents, so there is no rival for the father figure's love. Furthermore, when one child does make contact it is via a distant mode of communication. He exists as a disembodied voice, no more. Just a soliloquy in a room, ventriloquising through a machine. An alternative interpretation is that Harrow is playing through the distance he put between himself and his family when he was in Oxford.

But the blind man need not be a displacement of Harrow's father. It could be a projection of Harrow himself, someone who cannot find his way or someone who is scared to face his trauma because it threatens him with destruction. He would rather be blind and shun life than face things that would, in his unconscious fears, annihilate him. His inability to empathise also emerged. It was the striking self-centredness of, 'I, I, I.' His fantasy did not consider how anyone else would have felt.

Anna the dancer is another interesting, peripheral figure in Harrow's fantasies and I can't quite get her out of my mind. She came and went with no suggestion that Gonzago did anything to harm her, yet Harrow's sister Elizabeth was also a dancer. He seemed anxious about what happens to the dancer when she can no longer dance. Is he trying to stop decrepitude, thinking he is undertaking an act of preservation when he is undertaking an act of brutal destruction? Decay is inevitable. It is mutability. Harrow killed the dancer. He killed his sister in real life.

Or is the fantasy just illuminating simple jealousy, that he did not want to share his sister with anyone else? Even his best friend, George Gildern, was constructed as a rival in that regard, as was the newspaper photographer. And the distance, too. Harrow liked to watch the dancer but never wanted to dance. It is clearly voyeurism.

Other things. The children's playground, suggesting Harrow, as Gonzago, wanted to escape back to infancy, a desire thwarted by the hostile reaction of the child who spat at him. And the complexity, too. The fantasies interweave. He sees a cat after the killing of Lacy and thinks of a cat in a squat within a completely different story. I was also interested in his switching focus onto an anti-Macassar in the fantasy when he killed Lacy. It was as though facing the trauma was still too hard so he relocated his attention on something safe, something in which he had invested no symbolic value, but the issues still emerged in spite of him. Something clean and untainted lost its lustre and fell. Structurally, it is similar to the fear of the graceful and beautiful dancer getting old. It is also similar to his focus on his mother's arm on her deathbed, disaggregating his mother into body parts so that he does not have to confront the whole of the trauma.

I have never encountered such elaborate strategies of repression. Well, maybe once before. Something will have to give. The hypnotherapy is paying off but it is a high risk strategy, both ethically and practically. I need to keep my work on this case a secret and I need to retain control.

Harrow reacted unexpectedly during the hypnotherapy, standing up whilst seemingly still in a trance. It was deeply unsettling. I have never seen anything like that before. I need to be careful not to force him to face his trauma before he is ready. It is dangerous to push the patient too far, too soon, but the prospect of success and what it would mean for my career is more than I can resist.

A final point – schizophrenics are rarely violent, contrary to the popular perception. Maybe Harrow has been misdiagnosed. Harrow is performing under hypnotherapy; elaborately, brilliantly. Part of me doubts him and doubts his objective. Therapy is never one way and I have to be on the lookout for symptoms of paranoia.

Not the symptoms in Harrow. The symptoms in me.

Hypnotherapy – session #4

The count down from ten to one.

'Are you ready to tell me more, Gonzago?'

'I ran away to a new city, my wallet stuffed with Lacy's money. I saw an advertisement in a newsagent's window for a flat.

'The house was run-down and unclean. There was a bed in the corner covered with a thin, white sheet, and a fine dust over everything. A light bulb without a shade hung from the ceiling. I moved in straight away. The landlord, a middle-aged man with coiffured, dyed hair, took my deposit and first month's rent in cash. He shook my hand too firmly, smiled straight into my eyes and left.

'I went to a job centre and got an interview for a night porter in a small hotel. I told the manager I had spent the last few years travelling around Europe doing casual bar jobs. He offered me the post on the spot.

'I handed room keys over to drunk, middle-aged businessmen at two in the morning. Some of them brought women back with them, who left again half an hour later. The job

147

was OK for someone who wanted to be invisible. I got extra cash-in-hand for cleaning the hotel rooms. I bought a second-hand car to get around.'

His voice dropped. Quiet, almost reverential.

'I followed you, Victor, but made the mistake of writing a note and calling on you late one night. It was obvious from your first reaction that it was too much for you and too soon. It did not surprise me when you did not keep our appointment the next morning. I realised just how serious my mistake had been when I saw your friend, George, a few days later. He regularly brought back supplies from the chemist and the supermarket to your flat. He looked anxious every time he left. He seems a good sort, generous to a fault I would imagine.'

The voice dropped lower still, to a hoarse whisper at the back of the throat. The reverence vanished and malice sidled in.

'Keep an eye on your friends, because they know where the bodies are buried. I would certainly keep an eye on George Gildern if I were you, Victor. Devious little fucking man.'

His stone-cold eyes fixed on me for a second, unblinking. It was as though he was blind. He swallowed. The eyes closed again. He breathed audibly. The voice rose to its normal tone.

'I made a mistake; created a problem for myself. After the failed meeting in Oxford, I went out and got wasted.

'There was a woman in the bar. I did not get her name. We went back to her flat. There was a drunken argument with the driver about the fare as we stumbled out of the cab. We walked up concrete steps rich with the smell of stale piss. We went into her flat and straight to her bedroom but something went wrong. She was not crying out but whimpering, calling for her mother. I did not do anything, I swear I did not do anything, but I took her front door key out of her purse, let myself out and sprinted down the steps. I ran back towards the city. I flagged down another cab and went home. I stripped off all my clothes before collapsing into bed.

'I washed myself from head to foot the next day, scrubbing hard at my skin. I put the clothes I had been wearing into a bin bag and shoved them to the bottom of the dustbin.

'I did not do anything. We kissed. We talked. I am sure I did not do anything. I do remember the argument with the taxi driver over the fare, though. He called me a fucking twat. I swore back at him. Earlier in the evening I had found out that the woman shared the flat with her sister but the sister was not there. I think the woman tried to get me to sleep on the couch. I undressed but went into her room. She was trying to telephone someone, her fingers searching drunkenly for the correct numbers. I did not give her time to make the call.'

The voice rises. Harrow becomes plaintive, pleading. His eyes open wide and he looks straight at me.

'I did not do anything, Victor. I want you to believe I did not do anything!'

His gaze switches to the floor. The eyes shut. His voice drops.

'I spent Christmas and New Year alone. Nights at the hotel were quiet and I was able to get some sleep on duty. The reception area was littered with coloured lights and tinsel. I avoided the staff Christmas meal. I felt relieved when all the decorations were taken down but the hotel was deathly quiet in January and February. Just lonely, jaded salesmen passing through, and silent women in high heels leaving the foyer and walking back out onto the street.'

He fell silent. He shuddered. I counted back up from one to ten. We both needed to stop. He was all at sea. He had called me Victor. He was losing all sense of selfhood.

The room suddenly felt very cold. We both breathed loudly. We avoided looking at each other.

The room was dark. I could not see her face. All she said was, 'Mum...Mum...' It was not loud, not a scream, but disconsolate, like a small child with a pain that won't go away. 'Mum.'

All I could think was, 'She is dead. Mother is dead.'

Dr Field

Harrow had spoken, for the first time, about a sexual experience. But it was a truncated account of a loveless, drunk collision. There was no sense of any craving for intimacy. There was just a nameless, drunk woman. It was also a violent assault. His other mention of sex, with hotel guests bringing women back, was equally loveless, and at the beginning of the session he had introduced the character of a sleazy landlord.

There was no way for me to know if the incident with the woman was an actual encounter Harrow had had, or another feature of his fantasies. The event occurred at Christmas: Harrow murdered his father and sister at Christmas. It was more than coincidence. He was letting things slip. Maybe he was addressing, symbolically, what he did to Elizabeth. It was noteworthy, however, that the incident was on the margins again. Just a girl in a flat in an anonymous town, though with the odd detail that a sister might have been living there. Siblings are a constant in his stories but they are never on hand to provide support.

I checked Harrow's file to see if he had ever had a job as a hotel night porter. I could not find anything, though a small detail like that, not obviously relevant to his condition, might never have been noted, especially if it predated his symptoms. He had not said anything substantial about the job he had had in Oxford in his student days, so maybe that was the basis of the story. The fantasy also exposed repressed feelings about George Gildern, forcing their way out.

However, by far the most interesting aspect of this session was that he addressed me as Victor. I cannot be certain what is going on in that regard. His immersion in the character of Gonzago is total. It underlines the possibility that he does not have schizophrenia at all but, instead, Dissociative Identity Disorder. However, his file notes are weighted heavily towards a schizophrenia diagnosis, and the onset of hallucinations is earlier for Dissociative Identity Disorder than for schizophrenia. I will need to read his notes again in detail as soon as my time allows.

Tomorrow is my own therapy session. They have become the worst part of my professional life. Talking to another psychotherapist has ceased to be either cathartic or developmental for me. It is more like a game of cat and mouse.

Therapy can be compromising, too. I was conducting a session with a fellow practitioner who told me about an affair he was having with a patient. Clearly he was not the first ever to do so and it does not have to be destructive: Anais Nin had affairs with two of her psychotherapists and it never stopped her writing her books or having affairs with patients herself once she became a psychoanalyst. But, in my instance, my colleague's revelation put me in a difficult position. The therapy interface is sacrosanct and therefore my colleague's confession should have gone no further, but this was a terrible breach of professional etiquette, sleeping with a patient. It was exploitative. It was betrayal. I had a tough call to make.

I made the tough call. He lost his job and his marriage. Lost everything. His children stopped speaking to him. He booked into a hotel and took an overdose. He was found and revived.

He should have gone for another method, something more definite in its outcome, like hanging, or drowning at sea. Overdoses are often insufficient to cause death, and other would-be suicides make the mistake of thinking that jumping from a building will work but if they land feet first they just end up paralysed. The same goes for other forms of suicide. A coroner told me that people who jump in front of trains do not die instantly. They feel it. Their death is agony. Quite simply, most suicide attempts end in failure. You have to be certain about these things. Death is harder to accomplish than most people think, until the time is right. Ripeness is all.

A patient of mine hanged himself. I attended the coroner's hearing where they related the full details. I found myself imagining the death scene. The ripped-up bed sheets scalding his skin, the tight bulb of the knot bearing in on muscle and bone. The struggle. Legs flailing, thrashing the air. Gravity sucking the body down. The knot holding, fibres stretching.

The final, drawn-out crunch and the retching gasp of air. The pendulum swing of the body slowing down. The creak of the rope.

I had previously conducted my personalised hypnotherapy sessions on the suicide, really opening up his trauma, but had not told anyone about it. I covered my tracks well. I was exonerated by the coroner, hardly mentioned in the proceedings at all.

I had moved too fast with that patient. I must not make the same mistake with Harrow. I have to keep an eye on him.

As for drowning, no, I do not want to think about it. That is how Margaret – how Margaret died. It seems so fundamental to me, so ritualistic. The wilful absorption into the elements, like self-immolation. By fire; by water. There is nothing ambivalent about these kinds of suicides. They are for real.

I had another strange dream last night, a girl's voice calling for her mother, replaying an aspect of Harrow's fantasy. I did not write it down in enough detail when I woke up and now the lucid memory has gone.

Harrow's case is getting to me. Therapy is never one way. We start to see aspects of our own histories in our patients. Consciousness is formed, not fixed, and it can be reformed when we interact. It is a dangerous space for a psychotherapist to be in. I must keep my professional distance.

I have no idea what became of my ex-colleague after his attempted suicide. He just vanished from the scene. It was no longer my problem.

Harrow's fear of intimacy gets articulated through Gonzago. The 'I did not do anything' defence does not work. Harrow cannot cope with his desires and therefore he projects them onto his alter-ego who, ironically, cannot cope with them either. Harrow will have to be brought to face his trauma, somehow. He cannot get better, cannot re-enter society, without doing so. That is where I come in.

I should stress, however, that sanity is unattainable. It is purely an abstraction, or reification, pretending something is real and tangible. All you can strive for as a psychotherapist is to foster a madness that the patient and those around them can live with. We do not create sanity, just socially tolerable insanity.

I must remember to say that to the audience next time I give a keynote lecture. Not that I have any invitations in that regard at present.

I should also bear in mind that change does not have to be for the better. It can make things worse. A mental illness can be a survival strategy to fight off an even more disastrous outcome.

Harrow's fantasies in the fourth session have common denominators. They are comfortless, sleazy and characterised by isolation. He rationalised, through fantasy, his first visual hallucination by becoming the hallucination. In the final episode he started to describe sexual violence which was hard to listen to, but he has to do this if he is to move on. He has to accept his responsibility.

Harrow

No one ever found Gonzago. I know how that makes me look. But all the clues were there. All that was required was for someone to join the dots.

Tracking someone down is like academic work. You take all the clues, all the hints, you step back and you form a hypothesis. You test the hypothesis. You will probably have to make changes. You test again. Eventually you get there. Persistence, that is the key. He will be found, with persistence.

Dr Field looks like he needs a good night's sleep and a shave. Something is fermenting within him. He looks worried. I wonder what he sees when he sees me? I remember hardly anything of what I say in the hypnotherapy sessions but I feel drained afterwards. It must be affecting him, too.

I am getting more headaches. They come on without warning. The numbness is getting worse, too.

Hypnotherapy – session #5

'Are you ready to try again?'

'Yes.'

'You remember the handle, the gold handle, the deep breathing? The count down from ten?'

'Yes.'

'Feel OK about this?'

'I...Yes. I—'

'OK, let's do it.'

The slow count down.

'Gonzago, what can you tell me? You can pretend I'm Victor again, if you want.'

A shuffling in the chair.

'The following Spring, I felt ready and able to meet you again, though I still did not know the best way to do it. I went to Oxford only to find you were not there. I was faced with the prospect of coming away without seeing you. It was not good enough for me. I needed you.

'I left Oxford the next morning, drove under London and got onto the M2 into Kent, heading for your home. I was tired from the driving and had had a bad night's sleep. I pulled off the motorway, came to a dense woodland area, parked up the car and went for a walk. I found a river running through the wood, probably the Medway. I walked down to the water's edge. Apart from the lapping sound of the water it was very quiet. All the noise and congestion had vanished and I was under a clear sky. A pair of Canada geese flew past overhead, pummelling the air. I watched them shrink to small scribbles in the sky. The beat of their wings stayed in my head.'

Harrow's voice dropped.

'I undressed and waded into the water.

'There was another swimmer; younger, a boy. He saw me. He stopped mid-stroke and looked at me.

'"Victor?" he said.

'"No."

'"Then who are you?"

'He looked confused, even a little frightened. His question hung in the air, echoing all around me. Asking me who I was touched me on the rawest of nerves. It was a question that even I could not answer. It was the wrong question.'

Harrow stood up. I do not think he had any sense that there was someone else in the room.

'The next moment my right hand was on the crown of his head and my left hand was against his neck. I pushed him over and held him under the water, shifting my right hand down and cupping it over his nose and mouth. I pressed down on his sternum with the flat of my left hand. He kicked and floundered, waving his limbs around chaotically, sending spumes of water into the air, but it made no difference. As long as my technique did not falter there would be no contest. It was just a question of nerve and strength.

'The struggle ended. His resistance just sank and a final stream of bubbles drifted up to the surface. His life popped into the air and disappeared. I flipped him over and let go of his body. It drifted away from me.

'I had a beautiful, epiphanous moment. I felt as though I had baptised him. He was off to a beautiful, unspoilt kingdom. He spun slowly, a centrifuge radiating peace.

'I waded back to the riverbank and stood naked for a moment, watching him drift out of view. As he was about to pass from my sight his hand rose lightly on the swell of a wave, like he was waving goodbye.

'I got dressed and walked back into the woods. A little way along I saw a young woman, reading. I stopped and watched her. She did not know I was there, lost in her story. Graceful. I came up close behind her but, having made up my mind to speak, I turned and left. She did not move, staying as still as the trees.'

Harrow sat down again. He paused.

'I drove up to London. I stayed for a couple of days in a cheap hotel at the back of Victoria station. Prostitutes left their calling cards in phone boxes. People rented rooms by the hour. I took one of the cards. It had a blurred photo of a heavily made-up woman leaning her head back slightly and licking the underside of her top row of teeth. She stared right at me.'

The wind rose outside. Harrow shuddered.

'Doctor, I'm awake.'

Dr Field

Harrow had jolted out of it. I had not counted him back. He just snapped out of the trance as he described a pornographic image.

He looked confused. He asked for a break. It was a shame. I felt he had moved into the really dangerous territory, the space where, ultimately, he needs to be. However, timing is key. I cannot push the patient too far, too fast, despite my commitment to a rapid treatment programme.

The intensive bout of hypnotherapy sessions is starting to disorient Harrow, which may be a reason for his addressing me as Victor in the fourth session. I will back off for a short time and, in any event, I have conducted my optimum five sessions. He has acted out enough of his trauma. Any more would be too much for him right now. We have good raw material to work from. In my programme it is important that the patient believes they are in control and can take owner-ship of their own recovery.

His entire account under hypnosis is, I am certain, fabri-cated, or false memories. The fantasy of Gonzago drowning Jack Harrow plays through, figuratively, an actual event, right down to the detail of a young woman, presumably Katarina the au pair, being nearby. But he drew attention to how graceful she was, an attribute he normally applies to Elizabeth. Either he is conflating the two characters or Katarina is just a cipher for Elizabeth, who in turn, is a symbolic representation of his mother.

The cruel exploitation of one human being by another is a near-constant in his fantasies. The obvious scenario in the case of Jack is that he is working through his feelings about his brother's death by drowning. He makes himself directly responsible for the death. Perhaps he is expressing his guilt at missing the funeral. Alternatively, maybe Harrow. No, not possible.

Before I left, I asked Harrow if he was OK. He nodded. I took him at his word, left him alone and chased up some paperwork. I also requested a book on Jung from the university library, to refresh my memory on the Jungian shadow idea. It is a wide-ranging category but could be a useful lens in this case, especially if I back it up with a quote from one of Jung's letters. I need to start mapping out an article or two.

When Harrow is Gonzago the immersion is total. He has no sense of himself as Harrow. Gonzago takes over completely. It is his play within a play. I have never had a patient behave quite like this before. I may have to look further into the possibility of a misdiagnosis. Schizophrenia does not show up in brain scans but a significant number of sufferers experienced childhood abuse or poor family support. Neither of these apply in Harrow's case.

Harrow's brother died through drowning, as did my sister. Harrow narrated it through Gonzago, but made it worse. It became a violent struggle; a murder. Harrow was on holiday with George Gildern when it happened but he spent a lot of time by himself, trying to regain himself after his first explicit experience of his symptoms, the hallucination. Perhaps? No.

I need to leave that idea alone. The police and the courts dealt with the death of Jack Harrow.

I need to leave thoughts of drowning alone, too.

My own therapy yesterday. All over in fifty minutes. I tried to keep it in a relatively safe space. There are things I need to keep covered up right now. Some things are repressed for good reason.

I may have made a mistake. I talked about alcohol. The session did not go to plan. I gave away too much. She wanted to know what alcohol did for me. I said it turned the noise down. She asked if I drank with others; I told her I drank alone. She asked if I had any alternative strategies to alcohol. I told her I write things down a lot, my dreams for example, venting things in words to avoid venting them through be-haviours, like I encourage my patients to do. I did not tell her that I always think of the same person being my reader when I write things down. I did not mention any aspect of my childhood, nor the recent nightmares, about images of my hands on Margaret, pressing her down beneath the water's surface.

A death leaves so many unanswered questions. Margaret left a note but a note does not answer the questions. It just amplifies them. Margaret thought her death was an end, a full stop, but it was just an ellipsis.

I walk through the suburbs at two in the morning. Some of the streetlights are not working and there are hardly any lights on in houses. There is a lot of scaffolding.

How much longer can I do this?

Harrow

'Victor, can we pick up where we left off? I think we have done enough hypnotherapy, but if we have to we can do more, if you think Gonzago has more to say.'

'No, that was all he told me. I had something to say to him.'

'Ok, talk to me about that.'

We were in the pub garden. Gonzago's face twitched. I did not know if it was a smile or a nervous tic. He was claiming to be the murderer of my brother.

I tried to talk: 'What...do...you...?'

He cut me off. 'You wish I had never come into your life. This is too much for you to take in all at once. I understand.' Gonzago laid his hands out in front of him, palms up. 'But I need you to acknowledge me, to accept me. I could be good for you.' His voice grew colder and fell quiet. 'And don't take me lightly. I can make things a lot worse for you than I have already.' He raised his right hand and wiped it across his mouth. A smear of saliva remained on his lower lip. I looked down at my own hand: it, too, was damp.

What Gonzago claimed to have done would make him a sadist and a maniac. His face no longer offered any firm clues. His mouth was a flat line. His eyes gave nothing away. He was confessing to murder but Jack's death had not aroused that suspicion in anybody.

The air was still. The river lay flat and undisturbed. He looked into my eyes and said, 'Go back home, Victor. You need to. You're in no fit state to return to your research. Oxford is the wrong place for you. Go home to your family, Victor. Go home.'

I had only one question for him. 'How do I get rid of you?'

He leaned forward and whispered a word in my ear, his lips close to my skin. He stood up and walked away.

I sat for a few minutes until my legs stopped shaking. I did breathing exercises to try and slow my heart rate down. I walked out of the pub garden as soon as I felt strong enough to stand up and move. I headed back into town along the path by the river. My legs veered over into the hedge. The rough ends of branches and bramble jabbed me in the ribs.

I did not want to go back to my flat. I left the path and walked back along the road. I headed into the town centre and spent the rest of the afternoon walking around the colleges, not speaking to anyone.

As I swerved to avoid a throng of tourists on the bridge I heard his voice in my head say the word again, the word with which he had answered my question. The word was 'Japan.'

Japan. But no, it was not that. The word was not Japan. It was something that sounded like Japan. The word was there in my head but would not come out clearly.

I felt tears in my eyes. I was not crying because of a momentary pain but because confusion faced me whichever way I turned. I could no longer trust in anything: my family, my identity, my sanity. If I told everything to my father he was more likely to have me sectioned than to believe me. I had not done anything to provoke his suspicion or, at least, nothing that had been witnessed. Looking at the stars brought no answer, just a sense of unbridgeable space.

In the morning I packed as quickly as I could. I wanted to believe he was not real, that it was another hallucination but he had seemed real enough. He also knew a lot about me. He might have followed me. He might be outside my door again, waiting.

I crammed clothes into my bag. It bulged out as I slung it over my shoulder. I walked to the station, looking behind me and dodging the crowds, using back streets where I could. The word he spoke, whatever it was, still fermented within me all the way back to London.

Japan. Not Japan. Japan. Not Japan.

I got the underground from Paddington to Victoria. All the time I did not know if he was following my steps, or if he had been on the train at Oxford, or if he was crushed into the same tube carriage as me. I could not see him but that did not mean he could not see me.

On the train back to Kent I made a point of getting into the front carriage and sitting as close to the driver's compartment as possible, facing away from it so I could see anyone coming towards me and no one could approach me from behind.

It was late afternoon when I got home. My hair was unkempt and I had not shaved. The first thing my father said was that my eyes were bloodshot. I told him and Elizabeth it had been too soon for me, that I needed a longer break at home. My father clearly disapproved but there was not a lot he could do or say. He retreated to his study, pushing the door shut behind him.

Elizabeth just wanted me to be well. She busied herself making coffee and talked about other things. She told me about a man at work who wanted to go out with her. I wanted to know more but she did not go into details.

She went up to her room and put on some piano music. I could hear her moving, dancing. I thought about the way she lifted her arms, cupped her hands and coaxed the sky. A floorboard twitched and groaned.

I tried to watch television but could not think straight. The news was introducing an item about the Far East. I was scared the presenter was going to say 'Japan' and that everything was linked, but she paused and said, 'Taiwan,' looking straight to camera; straight into my eyes. Was that the word? Like Japan, it felt like it was close but not there yet. The word had more work to do in my brain.

Japan. Taiwan. Neither was right. It was like trying to catch my own shadow.

Alone in my bedroom that evening I tried to read some of my old books but could not focus. I had outgrown them and, in any case, my own research was surely going to obliterate them in time, if only I could finish it. I flicked through an undergraduate history of medicine textbook, took a different one from the shelf and read a chapter, pure pop psychology, on E.S.P., before turning out the light.

The word hit me the second I woke up. Trepan.

It was one of the world's oldest forms of medicine. A Bronze Age skull had been found in Palestine proving trepanation had been done at least two thousand years ago. A hole is bored into the skull, relieving pressure on the brain. And that what was I was being told. Trepanation would get rid of the illness and get rid of the hallucinations. All I had to do was physically unhitch the brain from the disease.

I waited for Elizabeth and my father to leave before taking a razor and scraping at the hair at the top of my skull, listening to the blade's rasp.

I took a peeling knife from the rack in the kitchen and scraped at the exposed skin on the top of my head, scrolling away a layer and gritting my teeth through the pain. There was a smear of blood along the edge of the knife.

My father always kept his tools in neat order in boxes and shelves in the garage, like they were catalogued. His drill sat in a plastic case. I clutched the handle tightly. It felt like the butt of a gun. I chose a drill of medium thickness, one of the longest ones, using the chuck to tighten it as much as possible. I found a bottle of white spirit and poured it over the drill.

I plugged the drill in the socket nearest to our large mirror in the lounge, squeezing the trigger. It whinnied and whined, spewing white spirit as it accelerated, screaming like a torture victim, whirling itself into a silver-grey blur. I let go of the trigger and the tension lessened. The screaming died. The drill came to a smooth halt. Pointing skyward, it looked like a spire or a place of worship. A call to prayer.

My hand tingled. I trawled a finger slowly along the drill's grooves, from tip to base. It was warm to the touch.

I grabbed a bottle of vodka from the drinks cabinet and took a large slug. I poured some onto my hand, too, and rubbed it on the shaved patch as an anaesthetic. I felt the sting across my scalp and took another large gulp from the bottle.

I thrust the drill up and thought of how a spear will always find its shadow as it arcs through the air and falls. I had hunted down my own shadow. I poised the tip of the drill over my exposed skull, craning my arm up high and bending my wrist. I must have been a little drunk because when I caught my own glance in the mirror I started giggling.

The right hand squeezed and the index finger tightened. My teeth ground against each other. The drill rose in pitch from a surly growl to a scream. I pushed down and felt the weight on my skull. The drill locked on and the point honed down, vomiting out shards of skin, flesh and bone. Rivulets of blood streamed down my face, finding their path like lava. My head rocked and shook and my teeth chattered. My vision doubled and blurred. It felt like the drill was static and I was the one spinning around like a blood-drenched ballerina. Bone gave way to dura mater, the outer layer of membrane protecting the raw, pulsing brain. There came a guttural, gurgling sound. Blood gushed out of the top of my head. Like energy, like pure life.

Brain cleft   in half.

A roar of sour heat escaping.   The bitter heatwave.

Abandoned neurons   tumbling away.

My right knee gave way, the drill whirled from my grasp and careened through the air, its own victim's scream fading, leaving a voice in the silence. My voice – out loud.

'Victor.'

    'Victory.'

        'Veni, vidi, vici.'

          'Vanity.'

              'Vainglory, glory glory, gory.'

                'G-G-G-Gone.'

I crawled on the floor, blood flooding in my eyes, soaking my face, seeping into the fine gaps between my teeth, dripping from the end of my jaw. I felt a peace beyond all understanding, a peace I had never known before.

A nurse in the hospital told me my drilling had made a new fontanelle, a new soft spot. The x-ray showed I had been precise and that I would heal, though a scar would remain. I did not need a blood transfusion, just time.

They would not discharge me until I had seen a psychiatrist. She looked like she had not slept for days, trawling her lank hair back behind her ear, rarely lifting her eyes above her clipboard. I told her I had been experimenting, all linked to my studies and my interest in psychology and unorthodox treatments.

'I know I've been reckless,' I said. 'It was a stupid thing to do. Maybe it was stress related. I'm nearing the end of my doctoral thesis, you see.'

She scolded me more than assessed me and made me commit to psychiatric outpatient treatment. She also advised that I stay with my family. I did not mind. I was sure I had accomplished my goal. Trepan. That was all it had taken. Self-trepanation to relieve the pressure on the brain and restore it to its natural equilibrium, its factory settings. My own hallucination, my own illness, had given me the right answer, the body's impulse towards self-healing taking over. Direct cranial diagnosis, intervention and treatment had shown itself to be effective, indeed decisive. I could be a case study. I had cured myself of hearing voices by successfully reintroducing techniques the established medical community had deemed to be heretical. I was going places. Bravo Maestro.

My father shook his head. 'I do not know what to do with you.' Apart from that he communicated with me in monosyllables throughout my first day back at home and kept to himself. Elizabeth was better but had started seeing her man from work. 'He has a future,' she said. 'He's going places. He's being fast-tracked. Drives a nice car, too.' I heard her singing. She did not normally sing in the house.

The man called for her most nights, parking outside the house and beeping the horn. Something stopped me looking out of the window each time he came around. Instead, I listened to Elizabeth's eager footsteps as she scurried to meet him and to the confident growl of his engine as he pulled away with Elizabeth inside.

It was my third evening at home. I was sitting in an armchair in the lounge, staring at an orange sunset. My father came in. He looked at me. He was clearly going to start talking to me again.

'Why did you do it Victor? Why did you do it?'

'I was experimenting, just experimenting.'

'You could have killed yourself.'

'I knew – I thought I knew what I was doing.'

A pause.

'You're hurting us terribly, Victor.'

It went on. He asked me, for the first time ever, if I was 'romantically involved' with anyone in Oxford. He stood close to me, within my body space, his stomach level with my head. I looked up at him. I was happy, indeed eager, to set him straight. I stressed the strength of my feelings for him and Elizabeth and the monastic nature of my life at university. I tried not to talk about the self-trepanation, other than to say it was the stupid impulse of a moment and I had overestimated my capabilities. My father seemed to accept my answers but he also said he was worried: 'You're so gloomy; so withdrawn.' He also, characteristically, drew attention to the cost of the cleaning. 'We had to get professionals in, you know. The blood. I had not thought there could be so much of it.' I glanced down at the pristine, smug carpet.

My father sat on the sofa and leant forwards. His legs were apart; his hands clasped between his knees. He was clearly expecting another response. I looked back at him. I hoped, believed, I had expunged the demon. I had taken the necessary if dramatic steps to resolve the crisis by addressing the illness in the brain directly. I watched my father's lips move and ignored his words as he carried on, waiting for me to interject. I nodded once or twice and flicked a smile. He stopped.

I leaned forward out of my chair, touched him on the shoulder and smiled, broader this time. 'I'm OK. I'm getting better. I'm sure.' He was hot to the touch. He smiled back and reached out towards me. I let go and headed up to my room, leaving him looking down at his hands.

Elizabeth was getting dressed for another date with her man. She stepped out of the bathroom with one white towel wrapped round her hair and another wrapped around her body and tucked under her arms. I stayed on the landing after she had gone into her room. The bathroom oozed moisture like a rain forest. Steam lingered. I could hear her moving around. I heard the hiss of a perfume bottle and ran back down.

My father had left the lounge. I started flicking hurriedly through TV channels, searching for anything to watch. I found a motoring programme where the presenter was test driving a sports car. I listened to the mellow self-satisfaction of his voice. 'She steers like a dream,' he confided, looking knowingly to camera.

Elizabeth came in. She was wearing a tight pink top and faded jeans. I looked down, noticing that my fingernails needed cutting.

'Are you watching this?' she asked.

'No, not really.'

'I may not be back tonight.'

I nodded.

Elizabeth pressed the remote control another couple of times and settled on a nature documentary. A colony of gorillas went about their daily business, described in hushed and reverential tones by the presenter.

The patriarch of the gorillas leant back against a thick tree. He gave a careless, desultory wave with his right hand. Two young gorillas wrestled in the foreground. It was play fighting, though it looked as though it might spill over into something more. Suddenly, one of the gorillas used his arms to pin his opponent down on his back. He sat astride him, threw back his head and cackled into the jungle air. I left the lounge, went upstairs to my room and lay on my bed, the sound of animal laughter echoing in my brain.

A car came to a halt outside the house. A horn sounded. Footsteps scuttled. The front door opened and closed. An engine purred, then boomed. I put my pillow over my head.

I was at a small farm show. There was a teenage girl. She was clay pigeon shooting. Her mother was next to her. They were trying to shoot at the same time, at the same target. The mother was overweight, stuffed into a two piece. The woman could not help but be aware of men looking at the girl. The girl shot at the wrong time. The mother snapped at her but it wasn't really about the misplaced shot. I watched them leave later in the day and made a note of the car registration number.

Dr Field

Increasingly, I can administer therapy to myself. I do not need anyone else and I certainly do not need a psychotherapist. I write my dreams down. I keep the written accounts together and, when time allows, group them, looking for common denominators. Working back from the symbols in the dreams I can identify what is causing me anxiety at any one time. As an approach it has a 'rear view mirror' problem as I see what is behind rather than what anxieties are necessarily current, but I can use the one to inform the other and all data is about the past anyway. I made that point in a seminar in my postgraduate student days. I could see everyone was impressed.

My dreams are about rivalries at the moment. Maybe it is a reflection of work, but the dreams play out rivalries between family members. Sometimes they are people I know, sometimes not. Sometimes Elizabeth features in them. The whole thing needs a bit more thought, especially as Freud was clear about the family being a site of sexual rivalry and jealousy. I suspect I am working through my own thoughts about Harrow's family.

Personally, I would have tried to stop Harrow from going back home after the self-trepanation. That was a basic error, in my view. Harrow needed to be in a clinical environment. Sending him back to his family was going to increase the likelihood of a relapse. The Harrow family was an environment that magnified Harrow's problems; it did not soothe them. An overstimulating social environment raises the risk of relapse in schizophrenia and Harrow was in a situation in which the father was inquisitorial and the sister had found a love interest. It did not bode well.

Harrow had recognised Gonzago's resemblance to him but was not taking the next step of recognising that Gonzago was his offshoot. It was Gonzago who was acting out Harrow's repression in an elaborate act of projection. Gonzago's appearance was Harrow's relapse signature and indicator. Gonzago was what happened when Harrow's repression strategies failed. He needed to recognise that his repression was ultimately self-destructive. Ironically, Gonzago gave Harrow good advice when he said Harrow had to acknowledge him. It would have been a significant step forward for Harrow to have done so, because he would have had to accept the existence of his own desires and thus move towards becoming a more fully rounded human being.

Margaret once said she could not be certain what person I was going to be each day when I woke up. I disagree: I think we both acquired set characteristics over time, settling into personae to take to the world. Mine propelled me into medicine. Her character took her elsewhere. Took her, finally, to a room with a sea view. The last communication we ever had was the Christmas card I sent her, a simple card from a packet, with a robin on it. I cannot remember if I wrote 'Love, Robert,' or 'Best wishes, Robert,' or just 'Robert x.' I wish I could remember. They were my last words to her.

Harrow

The next day and the next day and the next. No voices at all in my head. No hallucinations. No unexpected happenings. No Gonzago. Nothing at all. Just quiet recuperation and a sense of someone slowly getting ready to pick up where he had left off.

I had my first session in the outpatient department. They gave me a young analyst; I doubt if he was thirty. I told him about my research. He was eager to talk, mainly about himself. Someone walking into the room halfway through would have struggled to identify the therapist and the patient. I wanted to tell him about the benefits of self-trepanation but he did not seem keen to listen to that part, asking me instead how I dealt with stress, how I dealt with high expectations, how I felt about losing my mother and brother. The first two areas were easy. The bereavements, less so. I avoided saying too much about them. I knew where he was going to probe next time. He asked me if I was taking my medication. I nodded politely.

Elizabeth's romance was over. She would not say why she no longer had a boyfriend but my father saw an article about him in the local paper a week later. He had been assaulted at knifepoint by a hooded man. There was no robbery and no injury was inflicted but the newspaper said the victim was traumatised and off work. The police had released a couple of CCTV stills but they were fuzzy, just showing the assailant running away, none of his features discernible. There was an appeal for witnesses and a phone number to call. Local residents were asked to be extra-vigilant. My father read the report and expressed concern about rising crime rates.

I tried to make myself useful around the house while my strength came back. I had a clear-out in my room, donating a lot of books to a charity shop in town. I also sorted a few old clothes to throw out. My father suggested that the clothes might go to a charity shop too but I said there was no point, they were not in good enough condition. He tried to say more but I cut him off, left the house in his car and got rid of all the stuff.

I lit a small fire in the woods. Afterwards I poked around the ashes, ensuring that nothing significant remained. A spool of woollen threads from a balaclava I had thrown out was still intact at the fire's edge. I took it with me and tossed it out of the car window on my way home.

When I got back my father said he a surprise for me, that someone had called for me. I stopped dead in my tracks. He told me George had returned home for a break and was eager to see me. George had already called round and he and my father had talked. I breathed a sigh of relief and said how pleased I was.

Dr Field

Harrow asked if we could stop for the day. Maybe he felt the need to tread warily. Having stepped out of the Gonzago persona he perhaps felt exposed. I was content to trust his judgement and not push him too far.

Harrow seemed to find sex revolting, given his uncomfortable response to his sister's brief romance, the ending to which was disturbing and posed its own questions, but if Harrow had developed reaction formation (the most likely explanation), he was shunning the very thing he craved: normal, human intimacy. It seemed to me he was scared of his own desires and hence developed a cold, intellectual persona expressing the opposite of those desires. In particular, he was repressing a desire for his adopted sister. Meanwhile, the desires forced an opening through Gonzago. But even Gonzago's narratives were largely chaste. Violent, yes, but not consistently sexual. Some series of events must have steered Harrow away from the healthy pursuit of intimacy. The death of his mother was doubtless significant but I could not be certain that it was both necessary and sufficient.

Why did Harrow light a fire in the woods?

I know a lot of my colleagues find me cold and unapproachable, too. It is just a persona. I do not like to mix my professional and personal lives. If you put things in a box you can close the lid, at least for a time. Moreover, there are things I do not want to share, things that would get in the way of getting this job done.

That is something my sister and I had in common. She became cold very quickly. She changed a great deal. The development of my own persona was, I think, more incremental, though perhaps not everyone would share that view.

Next month, December, will be the anniversary of Margaret's death. Another year gone by but the impact does not lessen. The sting is as sharp as ever.

She took a small boat from the harbour and steered out into the bay. The boat was eventually returned to its owner by the police and Margaret washed up lifeless onto the shore. She was delivered from the waves face up. Her eyes and mouth open. A seaweed tress across her neck like a noose.

Harrow

The next day, too, was quiet. I thought about calling George but felt a headache coming on around lunchtime and had a rest in the afternoon. I excused myself altogether from the company of my father and Elizabeth in the evening by telling them that the pain was still there, adding that it was probably a delayed reaction to the trepanation. I took a couple of paracetamol.

I went to bed feeling troubled, expecting to have a disturbed night, but slept soundly and woke to a bright summer's day.

I was standing in the kitchen, looking out of the window at the light and dark green stripes of lawn and at a strutting magpie, when the telephone rang in the hall. I recognised his voice instantly.

'Will you meet me?'

'No.' My voice was barely audible and the word scraping at the back of my throat.

'Ah, go on, you know you want to. Anyway, I want to meet you.'

'It's not going to happen.' My legs shook. I leant against the wall.

'Did you think one drill would get rid of me?' His voice dropped to a hoarse whisper. 'Driller killer driller killer driller killer.'

'No. No.' Each word hurt me, snaking its way up my throat like vomit. I heard him draw a sharp breath at the other end of the phone. 'Do you think you can just return to your old life?' The pulse of anger rose in his voice. 'I'm onto you. I'm coming to get you. I'm going to bite you down to the bone.'

'Fuck you.'

'Fuck me? We're not through yet.'

His threat sent boiling lava flow through me, battering its way to the surface. I snapped like a grenade exploding. 'Just tell me where you are! Tell me where you are, right now and I'll come and rip your fucking face off! I'll tear you to fucking pieces!'

A pair of hands grabbed my shoulders and my body spasmed as though my enemy was right behind me. I span around to see Elizabeth standing there, her mouth open and her fingernails digging into my shoulder blades like claws. I held the phone between us. He had hung up. The dialling tone was audible like an alarm bell ringing far away. The phone dropped from my hand and clattered on the floor. My face fell on Elizabeth's right shoulder and I wept. I sobbed baby wails. I let go. Stale breath and hot tears flooded from me. She held me and rocked me, saying 'Sshhh, sshhh.'

Harrow breathed deeply a few times, regaining his composure.

The rest of summer 1990 passed me by. I was placed on a more intensive course of anti-psychotic medicines. I told Elizabeth it had been a prank call and I had over-reacted. I did not tell the doctor or psychiatrist anything about Gonzago. The pills they prescribed, quetiapine and diazepam, blocked out the worst of the anxiety and gave me long, dreamless sleeps, though I still had very little energy during the day, feeling tired after even the simplest of tasks. I put it down to the drugs' side effects.

The strength of my medication was scaled down in late August but I did not feel like I had recovered. I had lost all my energy and sense of purpose. There was a family discussion, during which I did not say a great deal, resulting in a decision that I needed more rest and a change of scenery. My father and Elizabeth said I needed to put my problems into perspective. I was clearly not ready for Oxford and being at home was not much better. The best period of health I had known in the recent past was during my holiday with George in East Anglia, until the calamity of my brother, so if George and I were to spend time together again there was a hope that my health and my outlook would both start to improve. It turned out that my father had already spoken to George and my psychiatrist thought it was a good idea, too. I was still managing to keep the psychiatrist at bay by talking about my academic work and what it meant to me. He kept probing at the deaths of my mother and brother, trying to penetrate me, but I fended him off.

To begin with, George and I went for a number of walks locally. He was the same as ever. Still smiling. Still unquestioning and uncomplaining. I wondered what his colleagues at work thought of him. Probably thought of him as the boss's spoilt son, or a mummy's boy.

George's father allowed him some limited time off work to help his old friend, and my doctor made further changes to my pills, giving me enough energy to take some decent exercise. I came off the diazepam altogether. Over the following couple of weeks we went on day trips to Kent villages, walking through fields and woodland and having lunches in country pubs, George reciting directions from his Ordnance Survey maps. It was good to pass the time just talking about the weather or the changing face of the countryside. Sparrows were no longer the most common of the wild birds. Instead, starlings swooped over well-manicured lawns at the front of quaint cottages. They jostled for position on bird tables designed to look like miniature houses. There was an obsession with cosiness wherever we went; people trying to wrap themselves in architectural cotton wool, fooling themselves that they were close to the soil. They believed they had everything under control when, in fact, they were little more than laboratory rats. I tried to discuss the issues with George but he could not see where I was coming from. He would shrug his shoulders, flash a quick grin and look down. Poor George. He really knew very little about the world. I think he was quite suggestible, quite malleable. Weak. My father, the clever lawyer, could have wrapped him around his little finger.

A couple of nights later, my father asked me what I thought about bird watching. He also asked if I would like a pair of binoculars. I wondered where he had got the idea from. It occurred to me that George was reporting back to him about my behaviour.

A number of things started to fall into place. George had apparently been interested in bird watching when we went to East Anglia but did not have anything to say on the subject when I tried to start a conversation with him during one of our local walks. The clicks were almost audible. George had been playing me all along. Not so dumb after all. Devious bastard.

For our most adventurous trip yet, we drove down to the Kent coast near Dover, finding a path along the top of the white cliffs. We walked in single file. A sharp wind made talking difficult. It began to get the better of George, slowing him down, but it thrilled me. It was like the current of life flowing into me again.

The sun shone fully in our faces. I looked into it, squinting. I could just about make out its perfect circle. I looked away and for a few seconds the countryside around me had the template of a feverish yellow disc placed on top of it, my eyes still registering the dazzling brightness. I turned around to see George looking at me. The yellow disc lay in the middle of his forehead, trembling a little. I thought about the time I had seen him posting a letter when we were on holiday. I thought about his closeness to my father. More clicks, more decoding; more falling into place. I wondered if he had come home of his own accord, or if he had been sent for?

'George?'

'Yes?'

'Were you…?'

'Was I what?'

'Were you…nothing.'

We stood at the edge of the cliffs, three hundred feet above sea level. Gulls and oystercatchers surfed the breeze. The tide fell back crisply over the stones below us, sounding like a volley of applause. It made me think of a line from Shakespeare, drummed into my head at school: 'The murmuring surge that on th' unnumbered idle pebble chafes.' Lulled into a reverie by the sight and sound, and by reciting the line from *King Lear* to myself over and over again, I started thinking about the randomness of life, how anonymous we all are, known only to an infinitesimally minute slither of other organisms on the planet. In the end, after a few, brief, accelerating years, we are swallowed up by the elements; not a trace of our individuality remains. The water closes above our heads and we are gone like we had never existed at all. Beneath our finery and our pretensions we are all just animals, scrambling to feed, reproduce and survive, getting through another day and imagining a glamorous future we will never have. Destined to fail and to pore the space between what we could have been and what we turned out to be. I looked all around me and stared into the horizon where the pale blue of the sky folded into the darker tones of the sea. None of this cared for us. I glanced across to the right at the main dock for car ferries and, beyond it, the smaller port for the Hovercraft. A memory flashed up of a sad girl with dark hair. I thought about her, how she moved gracefully, floating.

George said he needed to rest for a minute but I felt a strong urge to walk away from the path, down off the top of the cliffs and into the common beneath to see what was there. George said he would wait and that we would head back to the car when I was ready. I slapped him on the shoulder. 'You're a weakling, old friend,' I said. 'Darwin would have written you off.' I walked into the sun, scarcely seeing anything until I shielded my eyes with my hand. A gull laughed, taunting.

In the shade of the trees I saw large, grey stones ripping through the foliage. A scavenging crow panicked and made a loud, ugly shriek as I came too close. I sat down with my back against one of the large stones, oddly fatigued all of a sudden. I realised I was still a long way from health, as bursts of energy were giving way to deadening torpor without any warning at all.

I looked down and saw the mangled and bloodied body of a mammal of some kind, possibly a rat. By now it was little more than an amorphous splat on the landscape.

I suppose the tiredness got the better of me because I must have fallen asleep for a short while. I woke with a start, felt a sudden pulse of fear and looked around. It took a few seconds for me to gain my bearings and to tune in to the sound of the sea's distant rush.

I calmed down once I felt certain of the route back to George. It was no distance at all and, in view of the fact that I had dozed, if only for a few minutes, I was not worried to find the spot deserted. It was obvious George had started to walk back along the path and I only had to follow him. The breeze on top of the cliffs was cleansing, shaking the last traces of sleep from me. To the left of me lay the sea, sparkling in the sun. I started to sing: 'And did those feet, in ancient times...' I heard a siren in the distance.

The path began to head downwards. I could see the far end of a car park opening up in front of me as I rounded the final stretch. I was surprised to see a police car parked up and that two policemen were walking in my direction. I looked behind me. There was no one else around. The officer on my right stepped to his left as I came closer, so that they were roughly aligned with each of my shoulders. I thought they were creating a space for me to pass through. Instead, they asked me who I was. I told them. They glanced at each other and the shorter one asked if I would go with them. I did not think I had a choice.

Their car was not in one of the allocated spaces. It was right next to the path leading up to the cliffs. It looked like they had been in a hurry. I could hear more sirens, an orchestra of them competing against each other.

I asked what was going on as I climbed into the back seat. The upholstery was too hot and too firm, making me perch uncomfortably, and the top of my head grazed the ceiling. They looked at each other, for several seconds this time, before the officer who had already spoken turned to me and said, 'Do you know George Gildern?'

'Of course,' I replied. 'We're walking here together today. Is anything wrong?'

Again they exchanged a look. 'You'd better come with us, sir,' said the officer, sighing and turning to the front.

The room was cold. The floor hard and tiled. The walls bare. There was a large table and a tape recorder. The two officers were asking me a lot of questions.

I was shivering. I held a polystyrene cup in my hand, black coffee from a machine. I watched the steam waft up to the ceiling, making soft coils in the air. I imagined it as a barrier shielding me from them.

The door opened and a grey-haired, overweight man in a suit walked in, replacing one of the two uniforms. The man looked kind, smiling at me as he entered the room, but when he spoke his voice was aloof and stern.

He held up one of the uniformed officer's notebooks; a thick rectangular block of paper with a hard, light green cover. He said the officers had been speaking to witnesses. He asked me repeatedly about George and the circumstances in which we had parted. I answered him as well as I could. I asked to see George more than once but the man pretended not to hear me. I knew something was badly wrong and as each minute passed my sense of alarm increased. My requests to see George became more urgent. I squeezed the polystyrene cup; the hot liquid spilt over, running down my fingers, hand and forearm. I dropped the cup on the floor. Streams of coffee slithered into crevices.

There was a brief silence. 'Do you really want to see him?' asked the man in the suit. I nodded.

We drove in a patrol car, with the uniformed officer at the steering wheel. We arrived at a large building. The brickwork was a deep red, the windows barred with black blinds. We walked along corridors in silence, our shoes ticking on the tiled floor.

We came to a glass-fronted, cold room with white walls where a shiny, steel table held centre stage. A huge, piercingly bright light hung over the top of it. A crisp, white sheet covered the body on the table. All I could see was a range of peaks and troughs like a line of snowy-white hills. I seized up at the dawning realisation of what it might be.

'Ready?' I was asked. I could not reply, repressing a shudder. I did not have control of my lower lip and the words I wanted to speak died in my mouth. I nodded. The sheet was drawn back and I saw the lifeless form of George Gildern.

I stepped forward. His face looked like an aerial photograph of the moon. A patchwork of bloody bruises covered his face. He looked so frail. I gasped for breath, threw myself down on his naked torso and howled. My forehead pounded against his sternum. I butted him hard. His shoulders, neck and jawbone bounced upwards. His face juddered. His lips twitched. I howled with the futile anger of a starving child.

Hands grabbed me and snatched me away, fingers digging into me. My arms were pinioned behind me and I watched the attendant draw the sheet back hurriedly over the corpse. George's poor, white, cotton-clad outline was the last thing I saw before passing out.

I could have helped her career. Her dancing career. I'd have hired her out to small groups. Groups of men. Discerning men. No riff raff. Men of business.

I missed George's funeral. I found out later that his father had not wanted me or any members of my family there in any case.

I was hospitalised for more than three months in a private sanatorium in the South-West. I was placed on a course of heavy sedatives and do not remember much about this period. I was later told that for a month I was psychotic, condemning myself as the murderer of Jack and George and haranguing myself over the loss of Katarina, whom I also claimed was dead. I made constant references to someone called Gonzago. The doctors put it down to a post-psychotic state after an initial fit.

Once my rages had died down they moved me to a small ward. The other beds were occupied by poor souls trapped in their delusions. A man who thought MI6 were following him because of a book he had read. A teenager with long hair who spoke in rhyming couplets and kept talking about gathering up all the world's sins. Another man showed me a creased, black and white photograph of a woman cradling a baby. The woman had long hair and looked down. He said the baby was dead.

A nurse brought a trolley full of pills twice a day. An hour after taking them the patients fell back into their cocoons. My own pills were a cocktail of capsules and tablets. They made me feel numb and very sleepy. I gained weight. The nurses gave me regular blood tests.

Every time the effects of the drugs wore off I felt as though I had been placed on the edge of the cliffs at Dover looking out to sea, the wind whistling and shrieking around me and not a soul in sight, the temptation to jump overpowered by a dreadful loneliness, making me want to turn back and find someone. A lone seagull wove coils in front of me and wailed, its gullet mulching the air. It glanced across at me and I saw murder in its eye, as vicious as any snake. Waves hissed their white noise on the shore. Lips without a face slowly mouthed the word, 'Jump.' Each day I longed for the return of the trolley. It promised oblivion.

I was not allowed visitors. When I asked about this I was told it was for my own benefit, that I would convalesce more effectively without the excitement of family and friends. That is what they told me anyway and, in any event, I had no friends left. The doctors and nurses bombarded me with more and more drugs which slowed me down still further and reduced my speech to monosyllables. My jawbone was constantly numb. I would stand by a window in rare moments of animation, staring at the woodland lying beyond the institution's broad and pristine lawn.

In late-October I was slumped in a chair in the television room. I glanced out of the window. Thick bars of cloud hung motionless in the sky. I was watching a channel pouring out daytime fodder. It was some game show or chat show where all the people looked like catalogue models or shop window dummies. Their laughs were scripted. I peered closely to see if they were really breathing.

I heard a scraping sound coming from elsewhere in the room. I looked to my right and saw a familiar face. After staring at him for a few seconds it dawned on me: he was the plain-clothes police officer who had interviewed me after George's death. He was dragging a metal-legged chair along the floor. The rubber seals were missing from the chair legs. The chair sounded like it was screaming.

The officer sat down next to me.

'Hello again,' he said. 'Are you feeling better?'

'Not a great deal.'

'Maybe I can do something about that.' He paused and cleared his throat. 'We're not bringing any charges against you. It looks like your friend had a terrible accident. I'd like to offer my condolences.'

I turned and looked at him. He was holding out his hand towards me. It was a large hand with fat, cheerful fingers, but there was no point in making friends. I was condemned in ways that police officers and courts simply could not understand. He lowered his hand and continued: 'I came down to apologise personally for showing you the body. You were not up to it. If I had known your medical history and the stress you had been under I would never have subjected you to that ordeal.' I stared at him more closely now, puzzled. 'You've been through a lot,' he sighed, 'but hopefully it's coming to an end.' He put his hand over mine, enveloping it completely. He pressed down and smiled, the corners of his mouth rising up through his plump cheeks.

I heard another set of footsteps enter the room. A male nurse stood behind the officer, his white tabard starched and gleaming. 'Someone else is here to see you,' said the nurse, looking me right in the eyes. The police officer still clamped my hand down, the pressure pinioning me to the spot.

I tensed up, my hand trying vainly to pull away from the underside of the police officer's hot palm. I imagined Gonzago walking into the room, smiling insolently. Maybe he had another death to claim as a trophy.

'Who is it?' I whispered, barely able to form the words.

'It's your father,' replied the nurse.

The spasm relaxed and I almost sobbed with relief. The officer let go of my hand and left the room, nodding to me before he went.

In a moment my father came in and tried to smile but his face was as tense as steel. I stretched out my hand to him. 'This place is awful,' he said, 'and so bloody expensive.' He paused. His facial muscles started to twitch. He swallowed hard. 'Poor George,' he added. I could no longer hold back the tears at the mention of the name. I began to cry. I clubbed the arm of the chair. Poor George poor George poor George. I formed the words with my lips and repeated them over and over again until they became a mantra: p'jaw p'jaw p'jaw. I started to rock in my chair. The rage gripped me. I stood up, grabbed the chair and hurled it at the television screen. There was a fabulous crash as an explosion of glass shards sprang into the air. Sparks flew upwards like fireworks. The uproar attracted a flood of nurses. They bundled me to the ground and put me to sleep again.

I made a conscious effort to be co-operative after my outburst in the television room. I apologised to the psychiatrists and nurses, promising them I would work hard to get my health back. Internally, however, the image of George was forever in my mind, either standing on the edge of the cliff staring away from me, or as I last saw him on a mortuary slab with a battered and ripped face. It was hard to resist the temptation to shut down, and harder still to create a cheerful façade for the authorities. My only wish at that time was that final oblivion would wash over me like the tide, in one great wave.

In November, the nurses took a small number of us out for a walk. We headed towards the woodland. Autumn was well advanced and a few dead leaves wove around our heads in the breeze. The branches of the trees yearned towards the sky like the arms of drowning men. I made it as far as the fringe of the wood before asking a nurse if he would take me back. I clung onto his arm as he led me away, back to the brick wall sanctuary.

Alone in my room that evening I blamed myself for my feebleness, coming to the obvious conclusion that the sanatorium was a place of confinement, not cure. I decided to work as hard as necessary to secure my recovery and my release, conquering or at least suppressing the worst of my fears. From the next day I participated in as many therapeutic activities as possible, both to occupy my time and to convince the authorities that my recovery was underway. I had a new, short-term strategy: to get out of there at any cost.

My father collected me on the day I was discharged at the beginning of December 1990, arriving in the early afternoon. By this stage in my recovery I had undertaken a few supervised visits to local villages and towns, without incident. I had used my time conscientiously and was getting by with little or no attention from the staff. My medication had been scaled down. I had also spent a full day on the coast with two other patients and three nurses, hunting for fossils. It was a mild, windless day, the slow tide lapping over the rock pools. I found an ammonite, a softly corrugated spiral sucked back into a blurred centre. A hundred- and fifty-million-year-old souvenir. It belonged to a world more durable and patterned than the world I lived in, a world of beauty-in-order.

My father was happy to see me in what appeared to be a state of normality. However, I felt like I was being tracked, either by the recriminatory stare of George whom I had abandoned, however unwittingly, before his death, or by the calm, sneering tone of Gonzago. Each time I slept I replayed the moment when I had first opened the door to him in Oxford. My tablets, less ferocious than before, kept my fear at a just-about manageable distance but they could never expunge him from my mind's eye entirely.

A nurse gave my possessions back to me as I got ready to leave. Putting my keys and my wallet into my coat pocket felt empowering. I now had some money again, plus my college I.D. and my credit card. It felt as though I was tentatively rejoining life. I knew I had to try to begin again, or at least pick up the pieces of my academic career.

The journey back to Kent was long and dull. My father tried to raise my spirits by talking about Elizabeth, saying how much she was looking forward to seeing me. She had opted not to come down and collect me in person along with my father but, he said, a warm welcome awaited me on my return. The thought of Elizabeth did spark a mixture of affection and anxiety within me, as did the more general thought of being at home again. I asked my father if Elizabeth had found another boyfriend. My father shook his head. The road stretched out. I sat back in my seat.

My father kept his hands at ten o'clock and two o'clock on the steering wheel and never strayed above the speed limit. I spent most of my time looking out of the window, but now and again spasms would grip me inside like stomach cramps. I passed these off as physical symptoms caused by my medication but, in truth, I could have grabbed the wheel out of my father's scrubbed, impeccable hands and swung us both into the oncoming traffic. I was clearly a good actor, having convinced the sanatorium staff that I was better, but I had been

fooling them. Mine was a staged recovery, purely performa-
tive. It was possible that a lengthy rest at home would cure
me but, in any event, being at home offered one firm consolation. He would know where to find me. I had the guarantee
of knowing that either he, or I, or both of us would die. Our
next meeting would be our last. I would either kill him or die
trying.

The traffic started to build up and crowd around us,
hemming us in. We slowed down to a halt. Motorists put
their hazard lights on. The silence inside the car stretched like
cheese wire. My father put the radio on and found a station
playing classical music.

We edged forward to the point at which the hold up had
begun. I saw a caravan turned on its side and battered to its
bare bones on the hard shoulder, along with two crumpled
cars, their windows and windscreens webbed or shattered.
Night was falling: spotlights on tall tripods illuminated police
officers sweeping away the debris of a few more lives. Insects
zigzagged in the beams of light.

My father was exhausted and unable to carry on. He
found the first motel off the motorway and booked us a room
for the night. He lingered in reception to make a couple of
calls while I went up to the room.

It was like all hotels for businesspeople: stiff curtains, a
white kettle, UHT milk in plastic thimbles. My father came
in, undressed and climbed into bed. He was too tired for

conversation and just mumbled an apology. Within a couple of minutes he was snoring.

I opened the window and tried to think of my past as a bad dream from which I could move on but it was impossible. George was my victim: he would never have been at Dover had it not been for my problems and his best efforts to help me.

A voice shimmered somewhere nearby, 'Can you hear me, Victor?'

A different thought started to buzz in my head: that little shit George got what he deserved. The smug bastard got what was coming to him for spying, for reporting back to my father. One shove was all it had taken to get rid of him. He thought he was something but he was just a little management trainee for his father. A grin and a suit. He was fuck all. A car hissed past the motel. I snapped out of my trance and breathed heavily. Poor George. Poor George.

I thought about my ignorant childhood happiness, the death of my mother, my departure for Oxford, my mad enthusiasm for my studies fuelled by a desperate need for approval. I thought about Jack in the river, water swelling his lungs and rotting his limbs. An accidental drowning like that was a million to one chance. I wondered what had happened to all the grief that should have been expended. I thought about the night Gonzago knocked at my door. Four swift taps: fate calling me. A lot had happened in the build up to that night. A lot of stress had accumulated.

I checked I still had my wallet, picked up the room key and walked down to the bar on the ground floor. It was almost empty. I sat at a table in the corner and drank pints and chasers rapidly, staring at the artificial plants, blocking out all thought.

I was the last person to leave. I went back to the room and shut the window.

I awoke. It was still dark. It was also hot. I got up and tried to shake my head free of its alcohol cloud. I saw my father's jacket hanging over the back of a chair. There was a greetings card sticking out of his inside pocket. I took it out on impulse and carried it to the window. I held it up to the pane and could see, from the light of the yellow street lights, that it was a Good Luck card. I recognised Elizabeth's handwriting.

Seeing her writing made me hear Elizabeth's voice in my head. I thought of Gonzago and his threat to come and get me. His return was inevitable. If I survived, I would still have my loved ones. I would still have Elizabeth.

I could hear her voice and thought about her some more. I trawled my finger over the card, feeling its keen edge against my thumb. I went to the toilet and, finally, back to bed, slipping Elizabeth's card under my pillow, sleeping soundly.

We left the motel at ten o'clock, arriving in Kent in the afternoon. The winter sun shone all day. My father wore sunglasses for driving. He glanced over at me. His eyes were black ovals. He looked like a large fly or insect. 'You OK?' he asked, smiling.

The light glared even more harshly as we neared home. The sunlight emphasised every scratch and smear of dirt on the windscreen. My father sprayed the screen with detergent and the wipers swept all the mess away. I listened to them tick.

My father sighed as he pulled the car onto the drive and switched off the engine. He hauled the handbrake up and it groaned. I stretched, stepping out of the car, reaching up on my toes and pointing my hands in the air.

Elizabeth was standing in the hall, waiting. There were tears in her eyes. She was thinner, less voluptuous. The new look suited her. I thought about the time when I saw her in the hall after Jack had died.

The first day and night at home passed peacefully. My own room, my own bedding, felt luxurious after the formality of the sanatorium. The duvet cover had the warm, syrupy smell of fabric conditioner and did not rustle each time I turned over. The next day, however, the fear returned, creeping over me as the day advanced. Any time I thought about all that had happened a real insanity possessed me. I found it hard to speak or to look at anyone. My right hand had a mind of its own, slipping down over my torso and stomach until I clenched it and folded my arms. My body was threatening to revolt against me and I had to breathe deeply to retain self-control. On a couple of occasions I could have sworn

I saw someone move at the edge of my vision, someone fleeting. A man, possibly.

There was a new photograph on the mantelpiece in a metallic frame. It showed George in tropical surroundings in a red T-shirt and pale shorts, hands on hips. He was grinning broadly into the camera. The older photographs of Elizabeth and me still adorned the walls. My family's story was being rewritten. I wondered where I would get placed within the narrative. Not Prince Charming; that was faultless George, smug George. Maybe I was the villain or the fool.

I went to my room in the evening and thought it smelled unfamiliar, like someone else had been in there. I swept back the duvet and thought I saw a spider, but when I looked again there was nothing there. I ran my hands over the sheet. It was smooth to the touch, rippling as I moved my hand.

I hid my symptoms and my worries from my family as much as possible. I did not want to be sent back to the sanatorium. Only Elizabeth could draw me out of myself and help me relax a little. It was her voice.

Christmas decorations went up in neighbouring houses over the next few days, together with colourful strips of lights. The house opposite had a large string of fairy lights across its lounge window. Later that afternoon, outside a supermarket with my father, I reached out and touched a row of trees for sale, all trussed together and lined up in batches against a wall. The needles felt like barbs. One of them stuck to the sleeve of my jumper. I thought about how, within a month, millions of emaciated trees would be broken up, shredded and forgotten. It was all over too easily. It was the kind of idea I used to present to George, without success. He did not think that way. He was a simple soul. Stupid in some ways. Some might say he got what he deserved. He had been close to Elizabeth as well as my father. They had similar interests. I swept a green needle off the arm of my coat. I watched it fall to the ground and stamped on it.

Elizabeth put up our own decorations at home. She bought a real tree which she covered with baubles. She trailed lights along the branches. She took long streams of bushy, purple tinsel and draped them around the lounge.

'Do you want to help?' she asked.

'No thanks.'

'Sure?'

I nodded. 'I like to watch.'

She bent over, took a crib from a box and placed it at the base of the tree. She blew on it. Dust ran away from the baby Jesus.

The next day she went shopping for presents while I stayed at home. The Christmas cards piled up on our windowsills showing stables or robins or snowmen or a Madonna and child. A couple of them fell over. I left them there, wondering what or who had knocked them down.

On the weekend before Christmas my father said he was going away to a hotel in the countryside with some former legal colleagues for a couple of days of reminiscing. He told me Elizabeth would take care of me. A children's television programme piped merrily in the lounge. 'I know Elizabeth will look after you. She'll see to everything,' my father said. 'You are feeling much better, aren't you? I wouldn't want to take any unnecessary risks.' He smiled. I managed to smile back. Inside, however, fear seized me, the fear that Gonzago would take advantage of this opportunity to plague me again, when my level of protection was at its lowest. I looked into my father's eyes for a split second. They glanced back, showing no comprehension, giving nothing away. He did not know the risk he was taking. Both he and Elizabeth believed my illness was under control. 'Merry Christmas!' yodelled Basil Brush and his friends on the television. The puppet fox laughed.

On the day my father left my heart rate was rapid, as was my breathing. Self-control was harder than ever. I took an extra pill in an effort to calm down. Outside, the wind clipped dead leaves into eddies and whirlpools. My father made his preparations carefully, folding his clothes into his case. I suppressed my fear as well as I could and helped him to get ready, carrying his bag and slamming it shut in the boot of the car.

I had made my own preparations for his absence, making a mental note of the whereabouts of every long, sharp knife in the kitchen in case I was called upon to defend Elizabeth and myself. Whilst I wanted a confrontation with Gonzago, the thought of Elizabeth being involved was too horrific to think about. I had a primary responsibility to defend her, my number one priority. I needed to be prepared for whatever might arise, checking all the window locks. I was watchful.

I walked back into the hall as my father drove off, hearing the confident hum of his engine fade away. The wind died down, the low clouds steadied. There was silence, broken only by distant birdsong. I went to my room until lunch. We ate heartily.

We went for a walk in the park. It had become very mild for December. There were a lot of old people, some in couples but more alone. I watched the solitary ones; none of them seemed to know what to do with their hands.

The sun glared in our eyes until we were shielded by an avenue of coniferous trees. We walked one whole circuit of the large lake. The flowerbeds were bare but the grass had held its sheen, cradling tiny drops of water.

I turned to Elizabeth and paused. 'Are you worried about anything?'

'No. I just want you to be happy, Victor, and back to how you used to be. You don't have to say anything about it. I just don't want you to get upset. I am a bit worried about Dad's going away but I'm sure we will cope.' She was trying to calm me but I could see nervousness in her eyes. She looked around. 'Look at those grown men, playing with boats in the water. It doesn't take much to make some people happy.' I saw them; duffle-coated figures, little boys underneath the car keys and mortgages. They held big remote control panels in their hands. Their taut aerials hovered over the water like divining rods. A toy yacht veered over, the trim white sail slapping the water's surface. The boat flipped over, exposing the dorsal fin of its lower hull. A man's voice piped up, shouting, 'No, no!'

The sun began to fall. The soft wind shuddered the water.

It had become colder. We headed back to the house, hands plunged into coat pockets. Standing at the front door, looking up at my home, I sensed its stern solidity. I also felt the wind rise.

The central heating was already on. Warmth swelled in the hall. A slither of water gurgled in a radiator.

Elizabeth went upstairs to run a bath. I stayed downstairs. I looked through the French windows. The wind had become brisk again. The shrubs and trees swayed in front of me. Clouds shrouded the moon. Water drops spattered against the windowpane like a handful of stones and the sound of the falling rain blended with the running bath upstairs. It was far better to be inside.

The phone rang twice, then stopped. I took a few steps back and looked at it in the hall. It did not ring again. Instead, it squatted there on the three-legged table. Silent and smug. I smiled. I knew what the ringing telephone meant. It meant he had never stopped watching me and he was choosing this time, when I was unprotected, to return and, as he thought, torment me further. The phone call was the signal that he was coming for me again. He had used the phone before to get at me. It was not going to happen this time.

I went into the kitchen and took the largest knife from the rack. Its blade was broad, honing down to a rapier point. I turned it over and over in my hand. The lights on the kitchen ceiling bounced off the blade, winking a quick beam into my face.

I pressed the point of the blade against my thumb and saw a small bubble of vivid red blood ooze out of the flesh, forming a tiny, perfect globe before trickling down slowly into my palm. I licked my hand clean. I thought about trepanning again but knew how selfish it would be. I also knew how difficult it would be; I had gone into the garage on my first full day back home and had seen that the drill had gone. More urgently, tonight was not going to be about me. Tonight was going to be about protecting my loved ones, protecting Elizabeth. Gonzago had never gone away. I would have to get rid of him.

I had been wearing my winter coat while we were outside and still had it on, despite the heat. I put the knife into my deep, inside pocket.

I heard soft footsteps padding downstairs. Elizabeth came into the kitchen and stopped. She looked at me. I was frowning and my jaw was clenched. I could not help it. I was no longer in total control.

'Aren't you hot with that coat on? What's wrong?' she asked.

'It's tonight,' I replied, my voice struggling to rise above a hoarse whisper. 'After tonight everything will be fine. It's just tonight.'

She looked at me closely. 'What's wrong?' she said again. 'Have you had your tablets?'

I shook my head.

'Well that's the problem, isn't it? Let's get that sorted, right away.'

She stood on a chair and reached into the medicine cupboard high above the sink. I watched her body stretch up, the small of her back arching as her top rode up her waist. It was a dancer's pose. I wondered what she would be like when she stopped dancing. A middle-aged woman with a fine down on her top lip. Ageing would be a tragedy for her.

She brought down my pills and placed them on the working top. She filled a glass of water from the cold tap. I listened to the gushing sound. Outside, the rain kept falling.

Elizabeth passed me the glass. I looked down. The surface of the water was trembling. She said she was tired, that she would stay upstairs for a while after her bath and asked if I, too, would like to go to my bedroom for a rest. I held the glass firmly. I told her to go up, that I would be coming soon. I looked down again. The water in my glass had not settled.

Elizabeth went away, calling, 'And take your coat off,' as she walked upstairs.

I could hear the bath water tumbling out of the taps. I knew she was undressing, hearing her belt buckle fall to the floor with a clatter. I heard the bathroom door close.

I began to search the house. I was careful, looking for anything out of the ordinary. I checked every door and window downstairs to ensure they were locked and had not been tampered with. I peered into every corner, every recess in which a man might conceal himself. I took a torch from the kitchen cupboard, stepped out into the cold night air and scoured every inch of the garden. The rain plastered my hair to my head. It ran in streams down the back of my neck.

I walked into the kitchen and shut and locked the door behind me. I grabbed a tea towel and wiped my face. There was no one downstairs or outside. I climbed the stairs.

The bathroom door was open. I pushed at it gently, breathing in. The clean, flowery smell of Elizabeth's toiletries hung in the air. I opened my mouth wide. Steam cooled to liquid across my open lips. I walked along the landing, tendrils of steam lapping over my shoulders.

My father's room was empty. So was the spare room. I walked into my room, checking behind the curtains and under the bed. I swept back the duvet and flung open the doors of the wardrobe. Nothing. I stood still, hearing only my own breathing. There was no other sound: the rain had stopped. I was panting, struggling to keep a hold of myself, tense all over; ready for action. For a second I allowed myself to believe that I had been wrong, that he was not going to appear when, suddenly, I felt my eyes snap shut and was lifted clear of everything, as if by an angel. The glorious truth rushed upon me with all the stark certainty of a storm. I knew what I had to do and it had come to me in a blinding flash of knowledge: my epiphany. I opened my eyes to the truth.

I ran into Elizabeth's room and threw myself on her. She sprang up but I forced her down, jamming my hands around her throat. I squeezed as hard as I could, pushing my thumbs into the pit of her neck. A bellow rose up from my chest and soared with balletic joy out of my mouth, a cackling phoneme piercing the scented air above her. She tried to pull my hands away but her thin limbs were no match for me. Her eyelids flickered as her eyeballs rose gracefully back into her skull. With my right hand I drew the knife from my pocket and plunged it into the left side of her neck.

It was over. I rested my forehead on her collarbone.

I stood up and took a long look around her familiar bedroom. There was a box of peach-coloured tissues next to the bed and a tall, slender, diaphanous, pale green vase on the window sill. I looked at the tasteful, well-chosen prints: Manet's *Bar at the Folies Bergères* on one wall, a mandolin player drawn in pencil on another, Degas's *Dancer in a Ballet Position* above the bed. The dancer's eyes were slits. She was fringed all around by a grey and black shadow.

I opened Elizabeth's wardrobe and took out a long, old white T-shirt she used as a night dress. It had 'Choose Life' written on it in large black letters. I pulled it over my head.

I walked downstairs, stood in the centre of the darkened lounge and closed my eyes. I felt I was about to make sense of it all and that there would be no more confusion, ever.

I heard a scuffling sound, then a tapping noise. I opened my eyes. I looked at the window at the front of the house and there was Gonzago looking back at me: smiling, victorious.

I let out a soul-tearing roar of pain at the realisation that I had been betrayed again. I staggered towards the front door. My legs gave way. I pulled myself up on the door handle, tore it open and ran out onto the street. I stood in the centre of the road, naked from the waist down. The street was deserted and silent except for what sounded like the distant noise of running feet and a squeal of laughter.

I stood there, stung by the freezing wind. A drop of Elizabeth's blood trickled down my jawbone and fell to the ground, losing itself in the darkness. A light came on in one of the neighbouring houses. I turned and ran back inside, slamming the door shut and locking it. I kept running, upstairs and back into Elizabeth's room. I threw myself on her, wrapped my arms around her and kissed her on the mouth; tenderly, lovingly. Her lips seemed to yield up to me. With my arms around the back of her neck I shifted to one side and hauled my knees up to my chest, falling into a deep and restful sleep.

I woke to weak daylight in the room, saw what lay beneath me and vomited instantly. Her cold, splayed corpse, drenched in blood, some of it already dried and hardened. The wound in her throat gaped like a mouth frozen in shock. I peeled myself from her, a layer of blood clamming our bodies together.

Still hunched over her on all fours, I thought for a moment of all the calamities: my brother, Katarina, George and now Elizabeth. Only my father was left out of those whom I loved. I feared for his safety.

For the next two days I wandered around the house, never leaving. I ate when I needed to. I slept. I watched Christmas specials and toy advertisements on television. Bullying or coaxing voices urged me to buy an all-destroying robot or a doll who cried real tears. Fake snow fluttered down in the streets of soap operas. Reconciliations concluded dramas and comedies alike. Long hugs, wide smiles. Perfect families everywhere.

I did not wash Elizabeth's blood off my skin. Instead I let it harden and sail away in crusts and flakes, floating down to the floor. I did not dress myself but remained in Elizabeth's 'Choose Life' T-shirt and let my body smells take over hers. When the telephone rang I ignored it. It clicked onto the answer phone and I heard Elizabeth's happy, sing-song voice say that no one was able to take the call, along with an invitation to leave a message. Twice, after the bleep, I heard my father's voice. The first time he was full of bonhomie, probably a little drunk. The second time I sensed a note of concern in his voice.

I did not enter the room where Elizabeth lay. Instead, I shut her bedroom door, thinking it better to leave her in perfect peace. I lit incense burners to mask the smell. I watched the winter sun rise in the morning and I watched it set in the afternoon, all startling yellow light and no heat. None of this mattered any more. Time was irrelevant. All confusion had now gone and all outcomes were clear. The future held no shocks for me. I had crossed into a new space. I knew what to do.

On the morning of 22 December, the sun absent and an ash grey light hanging over the house, my father's key turned in the front door. I was sitting on a chair in the kitchen, staring at the ceiling. A delicate cobweb laced one corner of the room, with a spider suspended like a starfish in its centre. I heard my father's cheery call but did not reply. The door from the hall into the kitchen was closed.

I heard the familiar footfall of his steps up the stairs and realised he was glancing into our rooms. I heard him come to an abrupt stop. Swiftly, silently, I too walked up the stairs; the familiar knife in my hand, the handle nestled in my grip.

As I reached the top of the stairs he swung around and stared at me. A beautiful, absolute, pure horror stood in his face. I saw the unadulterated fear of death in his eyes. I stared into anguish, revulsion, the horror of the inevitable. Death in front of him, death reflected in his face. Death in the near-naked son before him, blood's war paint dashed across his face, grinning because he had crossed the bridge, because he knew death from the inside.

I raised my arm and howled in triumph as I brought the knife crashing down repeatedly onto my father's flesh and bone. The blade slurped as I yanked it out and crunched as I thrust it in again, cartilage and muscle trying in vain to frustrate the blade. The handle quivered in my grasp like it was alive.

My venerable parent collapsed like a detonated tower, the blood gushed freely and in a minute he was dead in my cradling arms. A new blood seeped into the pores of my skin.

I held him for a couple for minutes before allowing his lifeless flesh to unship itself from my arms and slither to the floor. His jaw dropped open on its tendons and he smiled.

I walked downstairs, went into the kitchen and switched on the radio. A choir of schoolchildren was singing:

Holy infant so tender and mild,
Sleep in hea-venly pe-eace,
Sle-ep in hea-venly peace.

I looked outside and, truly, it had started to snow. Have a very merry Christmas, wherever you are.

She hefts herself into another's boat and steers it out of the bay, the engine labouring. She stops in deep water. She breaks the water's surface with the points of her toes, her arms above her head. Time slows. The cold stings. The cold deadens. The weight of the water slows down shin, calf, thigh, pelvic bone. She does a final pirouette. Bubbles flume to the surface.

Dr Field

Everything I write and everything I do is for her but it is never going to be enough.

I tried the empty chair technique, sitting where I normally put my patients. I tried to imagine Margaret in the other chair.

I could not speak to her. I needed her to talk to me first. There was nothing but a chair and empty space but internally I was pleading for the space in front of me to say something, to give me something. There was nothing, not the faintest signal. I wanted a voice, her voice, to give me a message, to tell me what I should do, to hate or to forgive me. Anything.

Harrow has a voice, a voice that talks to him. I envy him for that. The other voice is from the unconscious, a symbolic communication from a deeper self. Maybe all it ever wanted to do was protect him. I don't know.

Harrow is delusional but he has not considered how useful delusions can be. Delusions give people a sense of meaning and order. We all have delusions. Some delusions are just more socially acceptable than others. The state of being delusional consists of nothing worse than holding a firm belief despite all the evidence to the contrary. Recently spurned lovers do it all the time.

If only I could

When I was young I

When I was young I thought nothing had consequences – wrong.

If I could do undo one thing, just one thing.

Fixed stars don't have to rule a life, but it is hard to free yourself from the trammels. It is hard to shake off the beam.

Cellularly, we become a new self every seven years. So why can't I build a new self? Each time I've tried I bring the shadow of the old self with me. The shadow needs to be hauled out of the darkness and into the light.

Harrow shivers. He seems spent. There was no Gonzago in the final outburst. Just bare Harrow, all the wounds on display. The assault on Elizabeth makes me think back to his earlier description of a one-night stand. That was all a fantasy. It was a displacement of the real assault.

The care home in the early stage of the fantasy could be the sanatorium. Gonzago's description of his bed at Mr

Lacy's was a displacement of Harrow's feelings about being back at home, reinforcing the hypothesis that Mr Lacy in the fantasy was Harrow's father in reality.

Harrow provided vivid details about his brother's death. He identified Gonzago as the murderer, but Gonzago is just an offshoot of Harrow.

And the phone call, too. There was no one there. I am sure the phone never rang. The key is Harrow's reaction to Elizabeth. He thought it was his enemy who had grabbed him, but it was his sister. She threatened him through his sexual attraction to her, an attraction he could never acknowledge.

Gonzago is Harrow's character, his play within a play. Harrow needs to stop performing and start living. He was still performing in his account, ending it like he was hosting a television show. Pleased with himself.

I cannot talk to Harrow. I can only sit here while he talks. He is in control now.

A swollen cocoon breaking open, its fibrous skin ripping. A creature within, unfurling. Its sodden wings craving light and air. Antennae twitching. Breathing. Free.

Harrow

'Is there more to say, Victor?'

I woke up in a cell. My arms were strapped to my sides and my legs were bound together. I did not mind. I felt warm and comfortable. The walls were no less cosy: padded, reassuring. I liked the fact that there were no choices to make.

The restraints on my arms and legs were taken off and I was brought some warm vegetable soup in a plastic bowl with a plastic spoon. I made a point of thanking the nurse. He avoided eye contact. He stood in the corner while I ate and took the cutlery as soon as I had finished.

I got exercise time with other inmates. It made me uncomfortable. The hint of liberty reminded me of Gonzago who had got away, free to move from city to city and spread his hatred while I was trapped in a locked building with towering walls.

One source of consolation was that I knew I wanted to live, if only to settle my account with him; to rid the world of him in a last, purgatorial act. I had acquired a sense of quiet determination and it kept me going. Furthermore, I did not allow myself to become in any way distracted. I walked in small circles and fraternised as little as I could.

They sent a psychiatrist to interview me. He was a tall, thin man with a receding hairline, large glasses and impeccable skin. His eyes, however, looked worried. They were unable to stay focused on the same spot for any length of time. I decided the time had come to tell the whole truth, in order that further victims might be avoided. Even though my story sounded incredible, I knew I could back up every claim and show that I was, in fact, another victim, not the insane killer they were making me out to be.

I warned the psychiatrist that my story would sound unbelievable, but I stayed calm. I told my story briefly but with firmness and precision, marking all of the dates with accuracy. He sat there, making the odd note and occasionally raising his left hand to his mouth. I left nothing out, ensuring the psychiatrist was told every brutal detail. I ended my account with the fullest biographical details I could supply concerning Gonzago, including his possible whereabouts, and asked the psychiatrist to notify law enforcement agencies so that the real criminal could be arrested without any further delay.

'I can pass on your message,' he said, 'but I do not know what can be done, without corroborating evidence to back up your account.'

'You don't believe me, do you?' I replied. 'You are not going to do anything, are you?' I felt the rage begin to rise within me with all the certainty of milk coming to the boil.

'No, it's not that,' he said, turning his palms upward towards me. 'I will do what I can but, in my judgement, viewing the matter evidentially, it's unlikely that the police will believe you.'

I began to tremble. 'You don't believe me. You don't, but I know it is true. The real killer walks free. He'll come back and when he does I'll be waiting.' I realised that I had stood up and was banging my fist on the table. I knew I looked crazy. I stopped. The psychiatrist tried to soothe me like a mother soothes a child, with slow, calm words. He told me I was still under the influence of a serious illness. I could not tolerate him for another second 'You fool!' I cried. 'You arrogant, condescending fool. You don't know what you're talking about!'

I heard the sound of a buzzer, turned around and tried to run from the room. Several male nurses came in, grabbed me, bundled me to the floor, bound my hands and feet and hauled me back to my cell. They slammed the door shut behind them, the sound reverberating in my head like a bomb detonating.

The only restraint on my fury during that time was revenge and the sense of focus it gave me. I was determined to find and destroy Gonzago and the quest galvanised my survival instinct, cancelling out the thoughts of suicide which other-wise would have claimed me. I had thought of carving into my own wrists, swiping crisply through the vein with a knife stolen from the kitchen, or tearing strips of sheet from my bedding and hanging myself. It would be a release and an ending. However, it would also give him victory. No: any knife I could get hold of was destined for one home only and I imagined the ultimate thrust of a blade, searing through the roof of his mouth and nestling in the grey sponge of his brain. I was going to unseam his head and burst his brain cells like bubbles, killing the bastard who had destroyed my life.

Doctors fed me a constant diet of sedatives. Lawyers and judges carted me through tedious procedures and slotted me back in a cell in a high security hospital. I was pleased to be rid of courtrooms, having no desire to be the star attraction in a freak show. I did not bother speaking. No one would have listened anyway.

I missed the family funerals. I found out later that my fa-ther's younger sister, who also took care of my father's will, had handled them. Back in my cell, a variety of psychiatric henchmen came and spoke to me once a month and asked me how I was. However, every question had a sub-text and I could see they were pursuing their own agendas, trying to create the conditions in which I would never be released. They had labelled me insane and they were going to be reluctant to admit they had got it wrong. They would deny me vindication if they could.

It was during one of these interviews, towards the end of 1992, that I asked if I could visit my family's grave. No reply was given and I was merely informed that the question would be passed on to the appropriate authorities, but when the next interview came around I was told that my request had been granted and I would be escorted to the graveside. I smiled and said thank you very much.

On a cold winter's morning, 21 December, a van collected me. I had not slept the previous night, becoming more and more tense as the first shards of daylight seeped into my cell. I dressed, ate, had breakfast and was hurried into the back of the van. The windows were barred. I was separated from the driver by a metal grille. I was also flanked by a guard on each side and handcuffed to both of them. They were large, silent men who stared straight ahead.

We drove south along the motorway, stopping at a police station for a toilet break. I could tell I was an object of curiosity for the officers and the civilian staff, a minor celebrity. As we headed into Kent I saw familiar landmarks: the Queen Elizabeth Bridge and Dartford's sprawl. Around thirty minutes later we left the main roads and lumbered through suburbs. Some of the houses were grey and dreary; some had solid, red brick confidence, bulging to the fringes of immaculate lawns. As I looked through the back window of the van I got brief glimpses of lounge curtains being swept closed in the late-afternoon as the world withdrew.

We entered the cemetery with daylight fading. A solitary robin hopped from headstone to headstone. We parked up and walked on. I saw rotting flowers strewn over graves in parodies of respect. The limp petals were just compensations for the real love that had never existed. A sorry scrap of a red rose, cartwheeling in the breeze, came to rest on the tip of my shoe. I watched it worry and tremble and fly away, a heart shape lost to the wind.

One of the guards held a piece of paper. He led the way, trampling across graves, row after row of headstones laced with spider webs. He found the family plot. I had not been there since Jack died. We all stopped at the same time. We were staring at the black, marble headstone. There were four names: my mother's had faded to a jaundiced yellow, my brother's was beginning to show the first signs of flaking. My father's and Elizabeth's still glowed with golden health. I saw the words 'devoted,' 'loving,' 'deeply missed,' 'Reunited,' 'Rest in Peace.' I knelt down and kissed the grass. My guards bent down a little with me but my arms were still stretched out behind me. Slender threads of green stroked my cheeks with the delicacy of immaculate fingernails. A dampness cooled my fringe.

I looked up and saw a glass vase filled with fresh flowers. They were marigolds, their orange and vermilion petals catching the last rays of the pale winter sun. I wondered who

235

could have put them there. I realised it must have been him, laying them here in order to taunt me. I knew he had done it deliberately, gloating over the bloodshed for which he was ultimately responsible.

I felt a pull on my right wrist. My guards were lifting me up. Still on my knees, I leant back on my haunches and catapulted myself headlong at the vase. I struck it firmly with my head, making good, clean contact.

Splinters of glass pierced my forehead, eyes and cheeks. My guards started swearing and shouting. I lay face down on the grave, the homeless marigolds draped across my head, shoulders and back, the welcoming grass sucking me down into the earth and dissolving me. I kept my eyes wide open and let the warm, rich blood drown out all vision. One of the guards screamed, 'Christ!'

It was some time after that before they relaxed my regime again. I was on suicide watch. An eye perched in the spy hole of my door at fifteen-minute intervals and peered at me as if I were the contents of a microscopic slide.

Once the authorities had relented a little and allowed me access to writing materials I spent my time devising intricate and well-reasoned theories about Gonzago's whereabouts and the means by which he could be caught. I passed them on to my psychiatrists, insisting, in turn, that they were given to the police. I suspect they were just added to my file notes.

Institutions are run by rules and once you understand the rules you can start to play the institution to your advantage. However, understanding the rules is not the same thing as hearing and acting upon the rules. The latter is simple: rules are drafted in a manner that means even the most stupid can follow them. To understand a rule, however, is to be able to decode the reasoning behind the words. I figured out what they wanted to see happen and did it for them. I enrolled for activities, attended meetings and took part in all the therapy sessions. I swallowed my medication. I made the very best of all the available opportunities for self-improvement and reha-bilitation. I made a spice rack in my woodwork class. The instructor praised it.

I began to gain the trust of the authorities. My conduct was predictable and irreproachable. I spent a bit of time with the other inmates, helping some of them with basic literacy and numeracy within the education department. The secure hospital was also praised for its horticulture and I spent many happy summer afternoons and evenings tending to the more delicate plants in the large greenhouses. Taking cuttings, mix-ing compost with vermiculite, dripping feed from a pipette; careful and considerate activities bringing new plants to life.

One morning, I asked a large young man who he was. He said, 'A murderer.' He declared it as blandly as if he was stat-ing his horoscope sign. I found out later that he had killed his brother. I helped teach him to read over the next few months.

He pored over the story of a farmer driving his tractor. The murderer's broad fingertips, riddled with black dirt, trawled slowly under the words with a scientist's precision. He turned and smiled at me on the day we made it to the end of the story without mistakes. His face was open and warm. It was the loveliest smile I had seen in years.

I expressed remorse at every meeting I had with a medical functionary. The psychiatrists were pleased with my progress. The doctors were content with my cheerful obedience as I took my pills. I attended carol services at Christmas and gave homage to the baby Jesus. The church altar was small, only large enough for the priest to stand behind. Its façade was made of horizontal strips of lightly varnished wood and was supposed to make us feel warm and comfortable, not intimidated by a broad slab of white marble. I did not mind; I could see what they were trying to do. 'Amen,' I said, gazing skyward.

Alone in my cell, I made good use of my time by reading as many great works as I could get hold of. One year I won the chess tournament. Slowly, I was being given more and more choices, like a dangerous dog being let out on a lead, link by link of the chain.

I was assessed by a social worker over a series of visits. She prepared reports for the mental health review tribunals. She recommended my transfer to a less secure environment. Subsequently, I was moved to a different hospital, in Hertfordshire. My levels of supervision were lowered over the next two years. The rehabilitation service at the hospital began to prepare me for independent living. I went on day trips, went shopping, bought my own lunch. All without incident, all with gratitude. The system was functioning efficiently.

In 2006 I sat through my parole hearing. The conditions of my release were strict but I accepted them with warm thanks, having ladled out my remorse to the panel. I moved into a hostel temporarily, avoiding the other residents as much as I could, before getting my own bed-sit near Nottingham. I bought a saucepan and a frying pan with my first social security payment. I also bought an old casserole dish which I never used and a second-hand radio alarm clock, both from a charity shop. I moved a couple of times after that, gradually heading north. I ended up in another bed-sit near Manchester city centre and waited.

The suicide attempt that brought me here was a stupid mistake. I had gone through a stage when the nightmares, especially about Elizabeth, were just piling up. There was nobody to talk to. I was afraid to mention it to my psychiatrist because it would raise the possibility of me being sectioned and detained again.

I woke up one Wednesday morning and it just seemed like the right thing to do. I was battle worn and wanted to surrender. I went to Boots and to the pharmacy counters of two supermarkets. I bought a box of painkillers at each, supplementing them with my prescribed temazepam. I had a lot of clozapine stored up, too, because I had stopped taking it due the side effects. I washed the whole cocktail of drugs down with red wine.

But instead of dying I just fell asleep and woke up feeling sick. I threw up, then felt cravings for water. Half an hour after drinking I would throw up again. This went on and on. I am pretty sure I had a fit as well, given the pains I felt afterwards in my jaw and muscles. I finally regained full consciousness on the Friday afternoon and ran to my regular outpatient appointment. It was obvious something was wrong. I had no choice but to tell the psychiatrist what I had done. That is how I ended up here.

I am not all that bothered about being back in an institution again. I am well looked after, with plenty of food and drink. There is no alcohol allowed but apart from that I could not wish for much more. Furthermore, there are good souls here who want to keep my strength up. They know the crucial mission on which I am engaged. The staff give me pills to ensure I sleep well and I sometimes dream about my father, Elizabeth and George, back when I was a small child. I am able to touch them and hold them and tell them how I feel. My father swings me up into the air and I believe I am touching the sky. I grin at the sun and it grins back. Little George, Elizabeth and I join hands and run around in a circle.

The thought of my release does not excite me like it should. Something is holding my hands down. It always has. It is as though I sabotage myself, will not allow myself to succeed. I had the world at my feet when I went to Oxford and look how I ended up.

I have bad times. There are periods when I know he has been nearby. A primitive form of telepathy operates between us. A seed of irritation nestles in my head, sprouting into rage. Gonzago does this as a form of torture, to remind me of his power. On the less frequent occasions when I dream about him I know it is a message, yet sometimes he is grieving and I know he cannot control it. I am getting a snapshot of his life projected into my brain. In his own way he is a prisoner too. No relationship is just one way traffic.

Sometimes in my dreams I see him in moments of happiness, buying a drink for a woman or sharing a joke with someone. Those are the images that drive me mad. Once, not long after the deaths, I dreamt I was on the edge of a lake. The weather was freezing cold, with a thin blanket of snow covering everything. A gossamer web of ice had formed at the edge of the water. Fog dimmed the landscape and snaked itself around me. I heard the water's surface part like a knife being drawn back along a whetstone and turned to look. His dead body rose up; the head, shoulders and torso bobbing on the surface. His eyes were open, looking upwards and to his right. His tongue lolled from the side of his mouth; long, broad and fresh-strawberry red. His teeth were bared, the lips peeled back, exposing his gums. I stared into his rictus grin. I woke up sobbing. I knew he had not died but I also knew he was suffering and I did not want him to die yet anyway. I wanted to be there when it happened.

I have started to fight back against him in my waking hours, telepathically projecting my own messages. I pour out my hatred, remind him of his crimes and swear revenge. I know this behaviour draws me to the attention of the medical staff and no doubt delays the date of my release, but there are times when I cannot hold back the anger.

The authorities allow me to mix with some of the other patients without too many restrictions. However, there are others who are kept away from me. I do not know whether it is for my safety or theirs. Sometimes, if I listen carefully, I can hear people shouting.

I am not the only one here who is on a mission. Some of the patients I talk to know things, too. They whisper to me. Snatches of phrases are passed between us. Even though the words are indistinct, the meaning is clear. These people are on my side. Together we will form a confederacy to conquer the evil that threatens us all. There are wrongdoers and tormentors everywhere, penetrating our defences, and we must maintain ceaseless vigilance to preserve whatever goodness may be within us, that the human race might survive and evil forces be beaten.

I know I must keep myself alive and prove to the authorities that I have recovered from the illness, brought about by stress, high expectations and extreme fatigue, which blighted my progress since my days at Oxford. I will secure my release and return there one day. I will complete my thesis and get an academic post, ideally one that is research based. Teaching would be a burden for someone like me. I do not have the patience to deal with people who cannot keep up with me. Most importantly of all, with my physical and mental powers back to the high levels I had in my youth, I will seek out Gonzago and end our conflict once and for all. I must be serious and focused. There is a life-changing journey to prepare for.

One danger, however, is that I am starting to lose track of time. A timetable is imposed at daybreak and lasts until nightfall. The days just replicate one another but the desire for justice never leaves me.

I am not naïve. I know that further obstacles lie ahead and sometimes the scale of the task threatens to overwhelm me. I have cried, alone at night time, watching the moon shine down on empty streets, the pale light tainted in dirty puddles. The sense of isolation can be enough to weaken my resolve. I was starting to feel desolation creep up on me but you appeared. You have renewed my energy because you have at least listened and you have allowed me to gather my strength for the quest ahead.

The time we have spent together has been important to me because my task is unfulfilled. If you are willing to do one thing for me, swear that, in the event of anything ever happening to me, you will take up my mission and take revenge on my behalf.

I know that is selfish of me. It is, I accept, unreasonable to ask you to devote your life to this task as I have done, but at least swear to me that, in the event of you meeting him, whether by accident or design, you will not lack courage. You must destroy him before he destroys anyone else. Be wary of him: he is eloquent and persuasive. He can charm you but do not be fooled. Remember the fates of my brother Jack, George Gildern, Elizabeth and my father. Remember your patient and friend, Victor Harrow, who has gone from being a high-flier to a fucked up psychiatric patient. Kill him. Bring an end to all of this. Please. I will be with you when you do it.

Dr Field

Article_v1

Psychoanalytic psychotherapists have long recognised the value of silence in treatment [insert refs here, including recent articles]. Furthermore, and in relation to child development, Attachment Theory has previously analysed how human beings in ~~family-like structures~~ families respond to traumatic losses, an approach which holds implications for the repression of trauma and [hence] for its treatment in therapy ~~interfaces~~ (Bowlby, 1999 [1969], [I will need to mention formative experiences between six months and three years]). In addition, in a seminal paper, Eisenstadt (1978) reported on the impact of parental loss on children, linking early loss with subsequent achievement.

This paper adopts a case study approach, with a subject with a history of voice hearing and violent criminality as its primary focus [possibly mention research ethics clearance briefly here, or leave it to a later sub-section, or omit it altogether – tricky]. The subject lost a parent in childhood [maybe stretching it a bit with Harrow because of his age – be willing to rethink], yet showed exceptional academic potential, as recorded by scores in UK public examinations, prior to his descent into violent criminality [more substantial subsection below]. [maybe start paragraph here] This paper argues that a pioneering form of treatment, combining the insight of traditional psychotherapy with the fast results of Cognitive Behaviour Therapy (Beck, 1979) has ~~significant~~ outstanding potential as an approach to psychoanalytic psychotherapy in cases of criminal madness.

Next section –

[Will need to decide whether to include Lacan. Harrow undertook radical, violent action against his father after seeing his reflection in a mirror and identifying it erroneously as his antagonistic other. Or possibly save for second article. Will have to ensure the scope of each article is tight.]

Another dream about the boat trip in the bay. It must have been the South-West coast. I remember the cliffs as sandstone, not chalk. The land in sight, the shipwreck, the bow sticking out at an angle. The rust on the hull. Maggie's hand next to mine as our own boat chugged.

Have to raise the ghost to kill the ghost.

A dream about a victim of drowning bobbing on the surface, head scrubbed by salt water. Bulbous and blood-latticed eyes glazed over. Bloated lungs. Seawater soiled splay of limbs and torso. All electricity in the brain quenched. All torment gone but with no vision to gaze on the shore. I woke in a sweat.

The loss of my mother was less graphic than Harrow's. And I was younger, twelve, and so entered a state of psychic closedown, leaving it alone until it was ready to be dealt with. I never got around to it. That was wrong, in retrospect.

My father just announced her death. The illness had been mercifully brief. He perched on the edge of my bed and phrased it as a broadcast, like a local news bulletin. 'Nothing to be done about it Son, so let's just get on with it. It's time for self-discipline. That's the spirit.' A rugged pat on the head. I pulled back my Superman bedspread and got dressed.

A core contention of Attachment Theory is that when a child is deprived of love in infancy it either becomes clingy later in life or it becomes cold. Just look at Harrow. Just look at me.

A child at the graveside. The space around him is galactic.

No more of that. Not now.

Harrow: an astonishing case. Obviously I have tried to keep my professional distance but I could not help getting involved. Therapy is intimate and therefore dangerous.

I have no doubt he believes it. He believes his fictional other, Gonzago, killed his younger brother and an old blind man. He believes that he, under Gonzago's influence, killed his adopted sister and his father. His self-trepanation was also prompted by the belief that it would be curative. There is also the issue of his role in the death of his best friend and his involvement with the family's au pair, but his file notes are no help in that regard. George Gildern's death was investigated by the police and deemed an accident, while no one seems to have questioned the assumption that the dismissed au pair simply returned home. His brother Jack's death, too, failed to arouse any sustainable suspicions.

I pressed Harrow about the biographical details of Gonzago at the end of the second and third days of his account, in an effort to start constructing a cure, or at least an amelioration of his worst symptoms. I wanted him to try to recognise his schizophrenia by showing him that, in the construction of Gonzago, he was projecting unacknowledged aspects of himself. I also wanted to see how much form and understanding Harrow could give to his shadow, in Jungian terms, using his fictional representation to trace back and illuminate his own trauma. However, Harrow gave me no details of Gonzago beyond what he said during therapy. When he clams up, he clams up. It complicates my treatment plan. I want to give him coping strategies but nothing springs to mind. I need to set aside time to read some published case studies, identifying what has worked before and aligning it with my own approach.

Harrow's visual hallucinations appear to have stopped but he believes he communicates with his loved ones in his dreams and, of course, his mental joust with Gonzago is never-ending. He still hears voices and talks of sending and receiving mental messages, which is a typical symptom of schizophrenics, many of whom believe they can broadcast thoughts or receive thoughts broadcast by others. Being able to classify his condition categorically should be helpful because it will give me parameters to work within and will make it easier to disseminate the work within the scientific community.

A further interesting feature of Harrow's case is what he did after he killed Elizabeth. He thought he was looking at Gonzago when, without doubt, he was looking at his own reflection in the window. He ran outside. He sought to pass through his own mirror image, his looking glass, after he had taken a decisive albeit criminal and brutal step. But he did not find himself somewhere new. He found himself where he had been before. He went on to kill his father. Nothing had been solved. Violence is not surgical. This is something I know.

Harrow notices men more than women. He described a psychiatrist with detailed attention to the psychiatrist's appearance. The only woman he focused on was Elizabeth, but he imagined what she would look like with hair on her top lip as she aged, becoming masculine. I have not given enough attention to that specific aspect of Harrow's case. There could be an element of repressed homosexuality.

I can well believe Harrow was considered a prodigy in his youth (his early case notes from psychiatrists back up his claims in this specific respect), which only increases the unique tragedy of his situation, as the impressive and effective subjectivity he developed is now surely shattered beyond repair. In Lacanian terms he encountered the mirror and smashed it. Years of bad luck for him, I suppose. Blessed, even cursed, with a powerful imagination in conjunction with a questioning intellect and sound analytical skills, Harrow could have achieved great things. Moreover, it is clear he did not lack ambition; far from it. However, it does not matter a great deal because he is finished. Maybe Harrow is, as he says, one of those people who self-sabotage. He would not be the first. I will give it further thought.

I should have made more impact in my career by now. My research is not of international quality. I do not get invitations to be the keynote speaker at conferences. Other people, they find it easy. People I trained with, they are professors now. They have big homes and high-achieving children. But after Margaret died I could not work for a while. It set me back at the period in my career when I should have been making most impact. Maybe I am angry at her for that.

Today, at the end of our session, I had to tell Harrow I would no longer be seeing him on a regular basis, although I will continue to oversee his treatment, which I will delegate down to junior colleagues (whom I will remind of my methodology) while I concentrate on writing up this part of my research. Further observation and analysis will be required to produce a comprehensive case history, but that can wait for now. I have to get to work, for my own career's sake.

Harrow thanked me for listening to him. He then said something else, which I wrote down pretty much word for word as soon as I left the room. He thanked me again and said, 'Our close family always possess a power over us. Our close friends, too. They judge us. I hear the voices of Elizabeth and George. Even if I try to force them away, they are there. But forget it, doctor. I have only one task now. I am sorry to admit that Oxford and all the other stuff is dispensable. My remaining purpose is to know that Gonzago has gone for good. Once that has been achieved, I can let go.'

Maybe. I thought Harrow put a slight stress on the word 'close.' He repeated the word and the stress. He might feel he let people get too close. I don't.

22nd November

I set myself high targets: always have done. I have determined to cure Harrow and do so quickly, but it will not be easy. His problems are more entrenched and more persistent than I had thought. The suicide attempt was less an aberration and more like part of a continuum.

Some things do not add up here. Schizophrenia is an understandable diagnosis and one with which I concur, but I have never met a schizophrenic as articulate as Harrow. It is not uncommon for schizophrenics to have learning difficulties and to score low on verbal I.Q. tests. That does not apply to Harrow but when he asked me to carry on his quest in the event of his death he exhibited an inflated self-conception, a delusion which is common in schizophrenia. It is also worth noting that a minority of schizophrenics are highly able. They are the ones who are more likely to attempt suicide. I can locate Harrow in that category. He already has one suicide attempt behind him, as well as the self-trepanation.

The research and the literature review done by my team indicate that general recovery rates for schizophrenia are encouraging. Only around a third of schizophrenics deteriorate irrevocably. Around a quarter have good outcomes and most of the others make a least a partial recovery. Up to a quarter of all diagnosed cases have one schizophrenic episode only and recover fully. Only around one in twenty commit suicide, though the figure is still high in relation to the general population, and some studies report even higher instances of schizophrenics taking their own lives. However, those generally encouraging statistics on the disease will only make my failure look more conspicuous, if indeed I do fail.

I must not fail. Must not. I must not allow myself to have thoughts of failure. I must cure Harrow and show that it was my treatment that caused his recovery. I must hold it all together. Must not think about all that other stuff. Must not.

Death by drowning. The desperation.

The anniversary of Margaret's death is not far away. The body was found by a dog walker. I can imagine the beast sniffing, snuffling at the sodden dress, at the upturned hand with the supplicating fingers like a surrender. The puckered skin. The softening bones. The dog licking its lips. A sodden mannequin. Not a human being at all. She was but now she wasn't. Not my fault.

Harrow's case might mean a great deal for my career. It could make me. I have known the Jungian shadow to be used as a metaphor for all the components of self unknown to and rejected by the conscious self. It is almost too wide-ranging but it might be a useful lens through which to view Harrow's condition and, moreover, it will allow me to include Jungian synchronicity, whereby the subject takes coincidences and ascribes meaning to them. Harrow does a lot of that. It is an idea I will need to work up for the article, which is proving very difficult to get off the ground, just like the treatment plan.

Nothing is happening, for some reason. That first clinical intervention will be crucial and the first paragraph of the article will need to grab attention. It is like I am clutching at something that is just out of reach, or which eludes me deliberately, like trying to take a hold of smoke. Furthermore, when I start writing I find other thoughts seeping in.

I have got to hold it all together. There is too much at stake. My career is on the line. I am just going around in a circle at the moment. I need to, must break through.

I remember getting the phone call about Margaret. It was as functional as when I was told about my mother. A female police officer said, 'Your sister is dead.' Maybe she said she was sorry. A lot of what happened afterwards is just a blur.

The same pattern in the dream, but the bay is deserted now. No shipwreck. The small boat's engine is stilled. We drift, Maggie and I. A slight swell. We rock gently. Red cliffs. The sky is like ash. I lean into her. The horizon tilts.

Article_v2

~~Psychoanalytic psychotherapists have long recognised the value of silence in treatment (insert refs here). Furthermore, and in relation to child development,....In addition...This paper adopts a case study approach, with a subject with a history of violent criminality as its primary focus [maybe mention research ethics clearance briefly here, or leave it to a later subsection]. The paper argues that my a pioneering form of treatment, combining the insight of traditional psychotherapy with the fast results of Cognitive Behaviour Therapy (Beck, 1979) has outstanding potential as an approach to psychoanalytic psychotherapy.~~

To include: Lacan (the mirror), Jung (the shadow)

This paper reports on a groundbreaking case study which has ~~outstanding~~ significant implications for the treatment of schiz of schiz

This paper reports on a

This paper

This paper reports

ground breaking

significant implications

This paper

I do not know why I did it. I was angry, but it wasn't OK. It wasn't OK, OK? At one of my therapy sessions she suggested I was angry at my mother for dying, could not acknowledge that anger because of the guilt it produced and therefore redirected the anger at another woman. 'Like Hamlet,' I said. She did not follow. I outlined the theory that Hamlet was furious at his mother for getting remarried quickly after his father's death, and to his uncle. He could not express his anger at his mother, his sense of betrayal, and consequently it got vented on Ophelia. It was cruel and Ophelia did not understand it. It was only when Hamlet confronted his mother that he was able to act, to overcome his paralysis. The problem was that the release of the trauma was too sudden. It unleashed a blood bath, with a signal at the end that the trauma had been discharged with Hamlet's last words, 'The rest is silence,' indicating that all the noise and the voices had stopped and the clutter had cleared. I had always thought the line meant there was no afterlife and no God but now I could see another possibility. Whether Hamlet is feigning madness or genuinely mad, he is like Harrow performing an alternative self in which the repressed surfaces.

Also, self-knowledge came too late for Hamlet. Had he lived he could have taken responsibility for his actions and tried to move on. He could have lived, he could have gone on. He wasn't stupid, just too self-centred.

My therapist listened. She suggested I was talking about Hamlet to avoid talking about the real issue. She said I did it a lot, used the intellect as a shield. She asked me outright if I was angry at my mother for dying, for abandoning me. I do not remember what happened next. I just remember being anxious about the session, anxious that she might tell someone else what I had told her. I was dying for it to end.

The suggestion that I am angry at my dead mother is ridiculous. I am not like that, not anymore. I am not emotional. If I am angry at anyone it is me. Just me.

Harrow liked drama at school. So did I. I liked the ancient Greeks, the chorus between the performers and the audience, guiding and translating. Some people are like that. They don't say a lot but when they do they shape us, cause us to look at things in a different way. A good therapist is like a chorus, translating the dramatised self for the observing self.

The ancient Greeks also argued character is destiny.

24th November

Pinning down Harrow's diagnosis categorically is much more difficult than I had thought. The early case notes show one psychiatrist saying Harrow has Dissociative Identity Disorder but I do not see it, despite Harrow's immersion in the role when he was giving Gonzago's story. It is not as though Harrow thinks he is both himself and Gonzago. He sees Gonzago as separate and as his antagonist. Gonzago was only present in the therapy interface thanks to my willingness to experiment with unorthodox treatments. The hypnotherapy broke him open. If only other psychotherapists would follow my lead. The profession would move forward. Once things become institutionalised they ossify. It is the pioneers, the risk takers, the rule breakers, who shift things forward. But it is also those leading the way who have arrows in their backs. I cannot trust anyone, either my colleagues or my patients.

It is possible that Harrow has Multiple Personality Disorder, but the root cause of MPD is often child sexual abuse and no evidence of that has been uncovered in Harrow's case history. The cleaving of the self occurs in MPD because repression is not enough. A more severe psychosurgical procedure is required, like two conflicting selves needing to be hacked and drilled apart. It is psychological trepanation, drilling into the space between two warring parties.

Harrow should have a review of his medication. He has complained of headaches and numbness. Most anti-psychotic drugs are bad for the heart and some can cause epileptic seizures. Furthermore, a lot of patients, up to seventy per cent, can be resistant to clozapine. In addition, if MPD did turn out to be a correct diagnosis there is not much point treating it with drugs. Unlike schizophrenia, MPD does not respond to medication. Only a talking cure will work.

I want to preserve this man. He is worth a lot to my career. I have to prove my standing in the discipline.

It is really hard to concentrate today. I thought about Maggie in the bay, the boat's engine ticking. Maybe she toppled over the side accidentally but I imagine her stepping in gracefully, the point of the toe lancing the water precisely. I think of a wave scything her chin and jawbone, the water smothering her, dousing and lifting her hair. The seabed craving her company, the limbs of weeds yearning to grasp her, coaxing her down. Did she hold her head up, tilt her chin, or just yield, desensitised?

A small room, rain in the northern sky and a life that's amounted to nothing. Rain falls on rain. Bruised clouds. ~~I'm sorry, but I have to~~ A door I've avoided opening but now I know I have to.

1st December

The heads of two departments have sent me a joint e-mail, copied to the chief executive and the secretary to the board of governors. They have taken exception to my methodology, my written records and my team meetings. It is possible that somebody has said something. I know better than to trust all the people around me. I am not a natural administrator and that is a fact. I keep meetings to a minimum and share as little as I can. Thankfully, the management do not know the full details of my treatment programme with Harrow. They would crucify me if they found out.

Maybe they have found out about the hypnotherapy.

It is important that I get the article written up without any more delay. I need to find a journal with a quick turnaround. The acclaim for my work will hold off any criticism here. I just cannot get any of it to happen right now. I cannot even get the introduction right. Each time I sit down at the computer I produce less. I hardly know what I am writing. It is like someone else taking over.

My team look to me for help and guidance but I have none to offer them. The tragic thing is, if I lose my post here (thinking of the worst-case scenario), all of my staff will lose theirs too unless they get relocated within the hospital, as the project will be brought to a premature end. The work is centrally funded which means all the power rests with management. I should have applied for external funding from a medical research organisation. I could have bluffed my way through the reports and carried on doing what I want to, what I need to.

My team are good and trusting people on the whole, who deserve better than this. That said, there are one or two of them that keep their distance. Maybe I am being spied on. It would not be the first time. People have stolen my data before, have stolen my ideas before, have said things about me to get me into trouble.

I am rapidly going off Manchester. It is cold today and the sky hangs lower than usual. It feels like it is compressing the air down. I find it hard to breathe. If I walk into the city centre I get jostled on the street. That is how it feels, anyway. I stay indoors, pour another drink into a glass that needs washing.

Yet Harrow came here and ended up in my care. Maybe I was drawn here, too, to be with him. I am beginning to think my encounter with Harrow was fated. I have been obsessing more and more about my own past. Both Harrow and I lost a parent when we were young. Both of us had an adopted sister. Both...

No more – not today.

I am going to finish that bottle. Start again tomorrow morning. Clean slate. The first day of the rest of my life. Everything will be good tomorrow.

Pull yourself together Robert. What did your father say to you? Think, what did he say? The important thing. Never go down in a street fight. Never go down in a street fight thinking they will lay off you. They will not. They will just keep kicking and kicking until you are finished, wiped out. Remember the boy at school. He did not fight back and look what happened to him.

I can feel it starting to slip away from me.
You need to wake up.
Think.
I never know what I am thinking.

Another dream from the same template. Opening a door straight out onto the beach. A cloudy day at the end of the year. The bay empty and the sea brittle as shale. Walking to the end of the land, stones snapping at my feet.

6th December

I went to see Harrow for a few minutes today. I think he can sense my unease. We hardly said anything. As I left his room I turned around; with the forefinger of his right hand he was counting up and down on the three middle fingers of his left hand. He was concentrating on his own movements, not paying any attention to me. Maybe he was trying to work something out. I would have asked him but I suspect there was no reason at all for what he was doing. As Freud almost certainly never said, 'There are times when a cigar is simply a cigar.' It is a true observation though, and so my considered, educated-to-the-bloody-hilt judgement is that Harrow was counting to three and back again to occupy the time. All I know is I know nothing. We are wrong to think extreme experiences are necessarily emancipatory. They do not always open our eyes and in some cases our eyes are better left closed.

Freud definitely did write to Einstein in 1932 and admitted that psychoanalysis was a form of mythology, like every other science. And do you know what? I agree. Just another myth. What's more, Jung wrote a letter in 1958 acknowledging the possibility of ghosts communicating with us. I do not believe it and doubt if Jung really believed it but we all have our ghosts, the things in our pasts we cannot accommodate within the world we have created and so they torment us at the liminal space between that narrow island of ours and the dark matter that could swallow us at any time.

I walked away from Harrow. I have my own problems.

As I was leaving his room I could have sworn I heard him whisper, 'It didn't work, did it?' I turned around, but he was looking down at his hands, staring closely at his palms.

I mouthed silently, 'I'm sorry, so sorry,' but he did not see me. The words stayed in my head for the rest of the day. 'It didn't work, did it?' A quiet, insistent voice, modulating. I could not be certain if it was male or female.

Whenever I meet a member of senior management they avoid eye contact with me and walk on. It is clear I no longer have their confidence.

All this has happened before.

Harrow

I wonder if he has looked at himself in a mirror recently? He has not shaved for days. His hair is greasy. His skin is dry, his eyes bloodshot. I can smell the drink on him, a sourness oozing from his pores. Whatever he was trying to do, it has not worked. It is like he has a wounded, limping dog at his heels.

I saw him standing beneath a bright hospital corridor light and his shadow was like a black pool under his feet. If I was him, I would not look in the mirror either.

I mentioned Dr Field and how bad he looked to one of the nurses. I mentioned the hypnotherapy, too. She looked surprised and left hurriedly. Maybe I said the wrong thing. I am sure Dr Field would be professional at all times, unless he is one of those people who self-sabotage. As a person he is OK. I would not want him to get into trouble.

I remember doing research with hospital patients. Professional distance can be hard. You find yourself feeling for them, despite yourself.

Dr Field

8th December

My room is filled with silence. The air is heavy. Breathing is hard. I am wheezing. I can smell my own sweat. I am not eating properly. My metabolism is bubbling all the time. When I do not feel hyperactive I get crushed by depression. Alcohol at least calms me down but I know it is not good for me and I have been overdoing it. I have been spending a lot of time in the pub, avoiding the company of hospital staff. My waste paper bin at home is stuffed full of blue cans. I am drinking the cheap and nasty stuff. It is not that I am short of money, not short at all. I just want to get drunk. Drop out of the world for a few hours.

I do not know about money, actually. I do not know what is left. I have not looked at my account.

The hospital management have already made a couple of my post-doctoral researchers redundant without any prior consultation, citing financial restructuring as the reason for their decision. This is dreadful and will require the reallocation of their work, thus increasing the pressure on me and on the remaining members of my team, but what makes me angry is the position Harrow has been left in. I recently sent an e-mail to the Chair of the Board of Hospital Governors warning her that, without my programme of treatment being followed through in its entirety, Harrow's health would decline. Of course I have been proved right, this is exactly what has happened and Harrow has pretty much withdrawn into himself. I am told he spends most of the day sitting in his room in a foetal position and is alarmed by any unexpected noise. He does not talk to anyone. He does not eat. It is obvious he is in serious danger of entering an irreversible decline. I suppose I should go and see him, see the truth for myself, but I cannot bring myself to do it.

I have not had a reply to my e-mail, just a one line acknowledgement from the Chair's p.a.

15th December

This morning, two members of my team approached me and asked if they could speak with me away from the wards and the laboratories. The three of us went to the staff kitchen. They were, in effect, representatives of the whole unit and they asked for clarification of their positions. I asked them to give me a couple of hours to gather all the information I could before reporting back to them, which left me with the unenviable task of approaching my line manager without a prior appointment. None of the hospital management are sympathetic to my work any longer. Seeking reassurances regarding the future of the project was more a question of hope than expectation.

The administrative block is at the opposite end of the hospital from the psychiatric wards. The sound of your footsteps bounces off the walls and the floors. I became absorbed in the noise. I was suddenly alerted by a brisk voice making a tannoy announcement, requesting my presence back at the unit. I returned straight away and was told by one of the office staff that Harrow was having a fit. By the time I arrived on the scene he had been restrained and injected with a heavy dose of tranquillisers and all I saw was a prostrate bundle of limbs beneath a human wall of male nurses. I was later told he had been demanding to see me and would have nothing to do with any other doctor or psychiatrist. It is a perverse vote of confidence I suppose, but it is doubtful as to whether this will have any effect on the senior management, who are moneymen rather than clinicians. Harrow is a helpless, pitiful figure and the nurses were crushing him. They gave him the liquid cosh and now he will be insensate for the next twenty-four hours at least.

The fit could well have been a product of the antipsychotic drugs but the hospital's way of dealing with it is to ply him with more drugs. Some of the most ground-breaking work of the twentieth century argued that a change in attitude amongst psychiatric nursing staff has more impact on the health of patients than any drugs, but no one cares about that approach any more. This is not about communication any more, this is not about people anymore. It is about systems and it is about a production line. Quite simply, psychiatric hospitals are an obstacle to recovery because they encourage social withdrawal and discourage patients from acquiring independent living skills. All I have ever wanted to do was to help people but none of this matters to those in charge. Drag the sick in under the Mental Health Act, flood them with drugs and spew them back out as automatons or zombies. A simple throughput.

It's not just my field, it's everything. It is all a question of brute force. Medicine, reason, morality, in fact all our claims to superiority as a species. They are jettisoned soon enough when one party realises it can beat another into submission.

The girl in jeans who sat with her legs apart, leant back in her chair and ran both her hands through her hair. The woman who asked me to snap my fingers along with hers. The woman whose phone calls I did not answer. They meld together and you realise it was you all along. You were scared of your own shadow, Robert, scared of getting into a situation where you could get hurt again and so you lashed out. You do not love and so you are as good as dead, but if you do love they kill you anyway.

But there's more to it than that.

She did not have to do it. I learned this from one of my private patients. He was a successful businessman, owned a string of restaurants in the North. He gave them different trading names and catered to different parts of the market, depending on the affluence of the area. Gino's served fish suppers in Salford, while Fra Angelico's served wood-fired pizzas to the wealthy young things of Alderley Edge. He had brought his only son up to be his successor and on the son's twenty-first birthday had given him twenty-one restaurants to own and manage. He created a chain named after the boy: Umberto's.

His son expanded too fast and spent his money too liberally, including celebrity openings featuring soap stars. His restaurants got into debt. The boy could not face telling his father that he had failed. Instead, he hanged himself.

I spent long sessions with the father who just returned to the same refrain, like someone who finds a hole and walks round and round it. 'I just want to tell him that whatever it was, it wasn't so bad. It didn't have to be the end. Whatever it was, there was a way round it. Whatever it was.' A handful of the man's restaurants still traded as cafés. Lone diners sat at counters eating lukewarm pasta. Paint peeled.

It was probably my weakest case because I resorted to cliché. 'What would your son want you to do? He would want you to go on, wouldn't he?' Would he?

In my profession we try to help people to move on. It is a con. When the trauma is a sudden death in the family for which you feel responsible it is a black hole sucking you in, exerting its own gravity. You are never going to get round it.

You just fall into it. The businessman thought he had seen his son in the street at night. I told him bereavement can cause transient hallucinations. I do not think he believed me. He had taken to going on long walks in the small hours, craving his son's ghost. Inspecting every shadow in the fog.

If the trauma isn't a black hole it is a whirlpool. Death by water, like Margaret. The incompressible water sluicing the sponge and passageways of lungs. A soundless death, a reversion to the original foetal curl. When my sister's sea-ravaged body finally surfaced, the tide shoved her coastward, homeward, into the air, offering her up to bewildered witnesses on the shore; dog walkers and retirees. Her limpid eyes looking skyward, the skin on her palms unfurling. I suppose it had to be that way, whatever it was.

A door swings open into a small hospital room.

'I'm afraid I don't have much time, Victor.'

'Good of you to have some to spare, Doctor.'

'May I sit down?'

'Sure.'

The chairs manoeuvre alongside each other.

'How would you assess your own progress thus far, Victor?'

'How would you assess your own progress thus far, Doctor?'

Silence.

'Victor, you haven't really spoken enough about the things you really need to speak about. You've only done it through another character.'

'Doctor, you haven't really spoken enough about the things you really need to speak about. You've only done it through…through me.'

'Victor, if you don't bring your trauma to life through language you will just keep revisiting it and it will just keep tripping you up.'

'Doctor, if you don't bring your trauma to life through language you will just keep repeating it and it will just keep tripping you up.'

The doctor crosses his legs away from Harrow, saying, 'I take it this is deliberate.'

A pause.

'Maybe deliberate, Doctor, or maybe fated. You and I see things in each other, things that aren't necessarily there. But they're still important.'

'Do you want to shadow, I mean mirror me?'

'Do you want to look in a mirror? No, didn't think so.' A sigh. 'Doctor, I'm finished. I'm through. The drugs only wore off yesterday and I'm covered in bruises. I've said and done enough. There is no hope for me. You're the one who needs to talk. You're the one who needs treatment. There's still time for you. You can make a change.'

A glance around at the door. A doctor swishes out into a deserted corridor. He bites the knuckle of his index finger. He swerves to avoid a nurse. She stares at him as he keeps walking. She clucks her disapproval.

Dr Field

16th December

It is done. I have seen my line manager and my project is being terminated with immediate effect owing, she says, to financial pressures elsewhere within the hospital, in conjunction with severe misgivings over my methodology and therapy. I will still write up my work but it will inevitably be imperfect. It is hard, very hard indeed, to take this. I was on the verge of something special but they have stolen it from me.

I do not know where I can go from here.

18th December

I am going to pack up my stuff, leave the hospital for good and head back down south.

Yesterday I was summoned to a senior managerial committee and was castigated for my work, which was deemed untested and unprofessional. They were all looking at me, their eyes boring into me. They said my therapeutic methods did not align with the research ethics clearance I had been given. They said there had been a complaint, 'a very serious complaint.' They made specific reference to the hypnotherapy. It is as good as accusing me of dishonesty. They may report me to the General Medical Council. It could wreck my career. I could be struck off. I was blamed directly for Harrow's declining health. He is refusing to participate in therapy with other doctors and is also refusing most of his meals.

The fools condemning me know nothing about psychotherapy. They are corporate men, passionate about golf but nothing else. They give themselves exotic and utterly meaningless titles like *business planner* and *corporate strategist*. It took a lot of effort on my part not to lose my temper with them, watching them shake their heads when they have no idea what they are talking about.

The last members of my team, conversely, were quite sanguine when they heard the news. They had seen it coming. They are all looking forward to going home, especially as it is Christmas. They have been very supportive with one or two exceptions and I will be sorry to lose them. They had a party. I did not feel I could go, opening another bottle in my room instead.

I have heard that Harrow's medication has been increased still further because of his withdrawal from therapy. I have seen him in the garden a couple of times, shuffling from one spot to the other, occasionally looking up into the sky but not showing any signs of interest in or engagement with anything. At his most animated he walks in a large circle. The garden itself looks uncared for. Tight twines of bindweed throttle the shrubs. The budget clearly does not stretch to giving people decent and dignified surroundings.

Harrow wanted to do great things but over-reached. He was too introspective. He should have realised he existed in a network of relationships in which he had responsibilities as well as rights. It would have strengthened his mental health and fortified him for the daily pressures of his role. Instead, Harrow drew the world into himself and it distilled into something bitter and mind-altering. His stress accumulated. It was too much for him to face and he could never discharge it, never let go. A mature awareness of those around him might have been enough to drag Harrow back before things got out of hand. He lacks insight into his own condition. He still does not fully accept that he is mentally ill; gravely mentally ill.

Harrow has his own gravity. Things collide with him. They scar him when he cannot absorb them. He lacks compassion, he does not empathise well and in asking me to continue his quest he has demonstrated a tendency to think of himself as a godlike figure aspiring to immortality, a fairly common trait in schizophrenics. What does he expect of me, complicity in his madness? Of course, he does not see it as madness. To him it is reality.

I worry about my own research, about how it can carry on. I have lost my credentials. No one will take me seriously. I may not get another job. I worry, too, about how the authorities found out about the hypnotherapy. It was between Harrow and me.

It had to be him that informed on me. The confidence of the therapy interface should never be compromised. That is a core tenet of my profession. He has betrayed me.

Was he playing me all along?

The nurses say Harrow's spirit has gone and his heart is weak. They are giving him pluphenazine injections in his backside. He is, I think, dying. The headaches, the numbness, the earlier fit: they could all be signs of something more serious. I want to tell someone but no one will listen to me any longer. What comment can I make on all of this? What can I say that could enable anyone to understand my feelings at this time, when memories return to haunt me, too? There would be nothing to gain from writing it down. I have tried already. Repeatedly. There is one listener in mind but she can no longer hear anything. Maybe my own methods are not effective after all.

What was it Hamlet accused his mother of? 'Honeying in the nasty sty.' Maybe it was 'over the nasty sty.' I cannot remember, like I cannot remember Hamlet's stepfather's name. Sometimes we repress things for good reason. We have a need to repress and forget. We have a motive. Smart people find an effective means of sublimating their desires and their traumas. Maybe I am not smart.

Sometimes, when we cannot cope with our own bad feelings and our guilt, we project them onto another person. It is not us who is bad, it is them. And we have all done that. Psychosis is just part of everyday life. Most of us contain our madness behind the face we prepare to meet other faces, but I have learned never to take a face at face value. The shadow is more expressive.

Harrow was just unlucky. His repressed trauma broke through to the surface but because he had repressed it for so long it overwhelmed him. I wanted to shed light on his darkness, but he has shed darkness on me.

My mind is itchy, sleep is difficult and relaxation impossible. I am drinking too much. When sleep comes I have nightmares or replay variations on the same scene over and over again, the scene of a boat in a bay. Sometimes I am in the boat. Sometimes I am watching and the boat is empty and motionless, and the sea is still, like dark glass, or shale.

I am going to head south. There is somewhere I need to visit.

Another nightmare — a face hacked by razor blades. My face. The used blade in a bowl of water. The strawberry red water.

A door swings open into a small hospital room.

A doctor sits down. Chairs scrape.

'It didn't work, Victor.'

'Didn't it, Doctor?'

'No. You're still here and I'm through. They've got rid of me. I've been sacked.'

'I'm sorry Doctor but maybe it's for the best. It seems to me you haven't been at ease with yourself.'

'There are things...' The voice fades away.

'There are always things, Doctor. Why not let go for a minute, sit back in the chair?'

Silence.

A boat rocks, expectant.

'I never meant for it to happen, Victor.'

Silence.

'Go on, Dr Field. Tell me where your thoughts are.'

Outside, a wind stirs. A handful of snowflakes stammer in the sky.

'You were eighteen when your mother died, correct Victor?'

'Yes, Doctor.'

'I was younger when mine died. I never grieved. I never got angry. It happened later.'

'Why are you telling me...What happened later?'

'I was just going round in circles. I never spoke and I thought if I never spoke about it everything would just go away.'

'It's unlikely that it would just go away, Doctor.' A pause. 'Have you stopped going round in circles?'

'No.'

A breath is exhaled, noisily.

'Tell me what happened, Doctor.'

'I was seventeen. I'd been having thoughts. Nightmares. Stuff about my mother was coming back, mad stuff, about her dead body underneath me.'

'Your dead mother? Her body under— But that's what I...I don't know what to say but, OK, so things about your mother were coming back. Well, they were always likely to. And?'

'I went into her room. Maggie's. She wasn't, she wasn't my real sister you see. She was my adopted sister. Not family. You see, you see the similarities with your case, Victor?'

'Yes I do. And?'

'She...We...No, I...Something happened. There was...You know, don't you?'

Silence.

'What did you do, Dr Field?'

Silence as weighty as a snowdrift.

'Afterwards. I went away. I left the house.'

'Was anything said, Doctor?'

'Nothing was ever said.'

'Nothing was…But there is still time. You can talk to her about it, or better still listen to what she has to say…She might…She might need to talk, to tell you…Or maybe it's best left alone. I don't know. There is nothing you can do to change it, Doctor. We all try to move on. Whatever it is, we all live with it somehow. We each have to take responsibility for our own lives. We have to. Either that or we give up.'

'No. No.' A raised and quickened voice. A hand smacks the arm of a chair. 'We have to bring things to life to deal with them. We have to raise a ghost to slay a ghost. That's my big idea, my idea, and they stole it. They stole it. And the only way to bring things to life is to create them through language, to voice them, because the return of the repressed is certain…Victor – Victor – I. She just lay there, crying. She called for our dead mother. She did not move, like she had thanatosis, like she was dead herself. And fifteen years later at Christmas she fell into the sea. She drowned. She died for real.'

A dead Ophelia rises to the surface. Language stops. A silence pleads to be broken. Outside, the wind aches and seizes a fistful of snow. The cold is as sharp as a slap.

'What would your sister want you…No, that's not it. I'm so sorry, Doctor. It sounds like your sister met with a terrible accident that Christmas.'

'It was no accident.'

'What do you mean?'

'She meant to do it. She planned it.'

'Planned her own drowning? What did the authorities say?'

'Open verdict. She had left a note but it didn't explain anything. It was more like a diary entry. I told the coroner I didn't know what it meant and I hadn't seen her in years.'

'Do you want to talk about the note?'

'Not now.'

Silence.

'If not now, Doctor, when?'

'Not now.'

More snow, tumbling and spilling outside the window like skydivers. Two men stare at the snow and at the ghosts of their own reflections. The world outside the window is like an old film, all grain, interruption and staccato movement. The world judders. The two shadows shift, reach out.

'I am so, so sorry Victor. If I could change one thing, just one thing.'

'You can't. It's odd, Doctor. You have your own shadow. You have your own ghost.'

'I don't believe in ghosts. Not that type anyway.'

'I think you do. Look. You can even see it from here. Look Doctor, look.'

Doctor Field is shaking.

'It's OK. You have to start the healing with tears, Doctor. Small children know that.'

A pause.

'You are right, Victor. Tears. Silence. Song.'

'You're accomplished, Doctor, and you're remorseful and remorse can be useful. Maybe you can administer treatment to yourself, be your own healer. You could start by being honest with yourself.'

Two men stop talking and look out of the window at the snow. A sob clutches a throat. A patient sees a doctor's shadow crumple and close in on itself. Snow falls. White flakes join hands in the sky and rest their tired souls on a bed of grass. Flakes flit like moths. Snow shrouds for an instant but the hard land returns. Snow dissolves on the heavy sea.

A body gets caught on the inward tide, comes to rest on the beach. A soft crunch of sodden flesh on tiny stones. For a moment the body looks like it has sighed. Its face gazes skyward and sees nothing like the blind.

Afterwards, she only looked at me once directly. A clear and knowing face. Knowing I had betrayed her. Knowing me for what I was. It is true that our deeds define us. I'm worse than the dead.

Harrow

I have tried to steer Dr Field. What he does now is up to him. He is still a child in many ways.

I have also listened to Gonzago for the last time and I know what happens next. The headaches and numbness. Fits, too, and now nausea. They all point one way.

I have told my story. I have gone as far as I can go. What I have learned is that a good death is an oxymoron, like free love.

Dr Field

I was trimming a grape vine. I went to clip the top of the vine with shears but saw a clump of grapes growing beneath a broad leaf, tiny and hard like elderberries or caviar, or like a clump of tiny heads. I pulled the shears away, hoping I had not stopped the fruit from growing.

Something was spoken. A beginning happened. There was a recognition, if not yet acceptance.

The water lifts. The boat feels lighter. At the stern the tiller shifts, listening to the tide.

I look out to sea, into waters I have not visited before. I glance around. There is a small rockfall, a shower of shale toppling, slapping the water's surface, kicking up foam. A sound like cymbals crashing.

Alongside the boat a broad wave laps back into the water, and bows. It closes; cadences.

My bags were packed in my empty office. I walked to the corridor of the psychiatric unit and went to the window to take one last look at the grounds below and hopefully get one final glimpse of Harrow. He was there, at the far side of the garden.

Harrow was standing just in front of the hedges. He was obviously in distress, his hands shaking by his sides, his whole frame trembling. I tapped loudly on the windowpane and called his name but he could not hear me. The word just echoed all around me. Suddenly, Harrow clasped his hands over his ears and bent at the knees as if he was about to fall over. I shouted out 'Harrow!' again and banged hard at the window. It was no use.

Harrow fell down. His whole body was shaking.

Harrow is dead. Brain haemorrhage.

Everything is done now. I am finished, through. This is the end of this story and it is time for me to go, to leave all this behind.

Gonzago

So...the rest...over and out.

Dr Field

The note Margaret left in her room.

I took a walk today to see all the debris of Christmas. The wind battered a strand of tinsel along the street. I saw paper hats, streamers and a condom all crumpled up in a bin at a bus shelter.

I stopped, out of breath. I used my inhaler. The bus shelter stank of stale urine, rich as creosote.

After the last arrest two officers took me to the station in a patrol car. A small crowd gathered in the foyer of the supermarket and watched me being steered out. I sat in the back while the offending bag of stolen wines was shut in the boot. The people in the supermarket blurred to faceless silhouettes all staring out from behind the window. Christmas lights flashing red.

The officer driving the car placed a folder on the passenger seat and so the other officer sat alongside me. At one point his leg was too close to mine.

The officer next to me told me I should speak with someone. How could I have told this awkward policeman that I had no one to speak to? I had spent Christmas Day alone.

We drove to the side entrance of the police station. The driver laboured out of his seat. The officer next to me opened the car door and held it while I stepped out, his right hand cupping my left elbow.

We walked in, me in the middle flanked by an officer at each shoulder. We came to a sealed door with an intercom on the wall. A camera craned over and peered down at us. One of the officers pressed it, a buzzer sounded and the door clicked open.

The desk sergeant recognised me. I had been in the same cell before. The door did not bang shut. Instead it clumped. A homely sound, a sealing in. I was left alone, sitting with my hands in my lap. There had been previous arrests where the other cells had been busy and I could hear shouting, screaming and crying, but this time there was only silence.

Later I was handed a bail sheet. I had whispered, 'No comment,' to all of their questions. The desk sergeant wished me a happy New Year.

I spend most of my days in a large old house divided into flats and bedsits. There is a row of doorbells outside, mounted on a rotting wooden board drilled into the wall. Two of the bells have been pulled out by force. They hang down, tired and dejected, the entrails of wires spilling out.

When I moved in, the first thing I noticed were the urine stains on the mattress like the outlines of carnations. A floral display to welcome me. The net curtains were a mottled grey and looked like tattered bridal veils.

I went to the window and looked down into the street. Large, unkempt and neglected houses. Lines of ivy growing like tendrils up the walls. I thought about all the people who had stayed here before, strangers who had just passed through.

I have a Christmas card in my room. A plump robin with his beak open. It is a couple of years old, the corners beginning to furl. I also have a postcard of a painting stuck to the wall with Blu-tak. It shows a girl standing behind a bar. She stares out, resigned among the champagne and beer bottles and mirrors. I have another postcard, too, of a girl floating face up in a river.

My brother always assumed I had settled down permanently with someone. Maybe I gave that impression in one of the few letters I wrote. As if that could be possible. I have heard it said that adopted children can find it hard to create good relationships later in life. It's true, for me at least.

Robert and I spent too much time together. We were too close. And our mother had died. And the family was insular, so insular.

As a child, on holiday, I would build a sandcastle close to the sea and count how many waves it took to topple over. It was entirely random – wave number nineteen might leave it intact but twenty might bring it down. Or twenty-one, or twenty-two. Robert hunted for fossils and I built castles. He would give me fossils but I had nothing to give. When I picture the scene it is just the two of us.

I tried. I tried marriage for a handful of lost years but we were just two strangers living under one roof. The marriage got mislaid somewhere.

The lump in my throat hardens.

I find it difficult to speak. When he came into my room that night, into my room, I called for our dead mother.

'Mum,' I called, but she did not come.

No one.

That's when you grow up, when you realise no one is coming and no one is going to save you. That's the moment you grow up.

I pretended I was a seashell, complete in itself and inviolable. I was a seashell, free of all desire. I tried not to breathe. No one can get at me now. It brought back the memories of when I was a little girl, before I joined the Harrows.

The weather was terrible on my journey to the coast. Sleet battered the windows of the train and we were held up at several stations. I booked in for one night at a bed and breakfast, telling the hotelier I was visiting family.

I have somewhere to go.

No, that's not it. The truth is I'm through.

Like him, I cannot run away from my past forever and, like him, I am dragged down into the dust by the memory of the evening when two teenagers struggled on a mattress and he shattered both of us.

Afterwards, he stood up. I was surprised by how clumsy and foolish he looked with his arms hanging down by his sides.

The following days were strange. The resolute, monastic silence. The avoidance of all eye contact. He left soon after.

I remember almost nothing about those few moments but I remember the clothes he was wearing. I never saw him wearing them again.

I am going to turn the heater off in my room. I will head into the sea, get cut by the winter wind, feel the cold sting of waves. I will walk past the 'Warning to Bathers' sign. The sign torn like the sea. The sea torn like the sign.

Water is the great silencer.

I will steal one of the launch boats, steer out into the bay, listen to the cry of gulls. I will head into the sea, my tresses will lift and it will be over.

'Who's there?'

'You already know.'

'I know.'

'Yes, you always knew.'

'I always knew.'

'Were you expecting me?'

'I knew you had to come eventually.'

'Are there others here?'

'There are always others here.'

A breath.

'Do you need help?'

'I don't think so. Not anymore. I can do things by myself.'

'What can you see?'

'Paths. A river trailing away with fields either side. But it's not silent here. The water is flowing, quickening, purling over rocks and there's a fresh breeze. I can feel it on my face. I think I'm prospecting for gold.'

'Time to go.'

Someone flicks a radio off.

Dr Robert Field

The silence after the phone call. 'Your sister is dead.' Each dust mote seemed painfully alive. Dogs, horses, rats all had life, but not her.

I remember it was raining. I went for a walk in a forest. Before that day I had never noticed the tonal difference in the fall of each raindrop. They nestled in the cups of leaves, they thwacked against tree bark, they muffled in the grass.

But, like Victor Harrow taught me, that is the past and I cannot change it. I can only take responsibility for it. I believe I am ready to move on. Maybe I could practise psychotherapy abroad or have a change of career. Something looking out rather than in, creating something in the world. I could train in horticulture or get a boat. But I must, I can, begin to let go. I can let go. I can let go of the rope, let the sail billow. I can head out into the sea where each wave is unique, where water backflips, all sinew and movement. I can pause and look into the depths, trawl my hand in the water, feel the cold, insistent tug on my fingertips. Not forget. What I've done is always there. It defines my character and character is destiny. Fate.

Is there ever a resolution? No, not for me.

But to go on, endure, is the only option, and you get to see things you would otherwise never have seen. It's consolation. What we do is what matters, but words, for all their limitations, can heal because they allow us to reimagine. Language does not reflect the world, it creates it. If we aim language at healing it can heal but it needs to be indirect because we have to catch trauma off guard. It is hard to trap a shadow. The shadow yearns and shudders to be elsewhere because it's a shadow.

There are graves to visit. Margaret's grave first. Harrow's grave later. It turns out I have been writing to Margaret all along. It cannot change anything but it is all I have left of her.

What was it Anais Nin said? Something to the effect that there came a time when the risk of remaining tightly wound in a bud was less than the risk of blossoming. That time is now. I do not need to live in my own head any longer. I am unfrozen, unfurling. I might meet someone. A page waits to be written. There is no shadow without the sun. A small boat rocks keenly in the harbour and someone, somewhere lets me go, releases me, from me.

Michael Flavin is Reader in Global Education at King's College London. He holds a degree, three MAs and two PhDs. He is the author of two books on nineteenth-century literature, two on technology, and a previous novel *One Small Step* (Vulpine 2022). He lives in Canterbury.

One Small Step

On 21st November 1974, a boy's life is blown apart. What comes out of the rubble?

Danny Cronin is a ten-year-old boy from a Northern Irish Catholic family living in Birmingham, far away from The Troubles. Danny wants to be an astronaut when he grows up and writes science-fiction stories with himself as the hero.

The Troubles come to Birmingham. Two bombs, planted by the IRA, explode in two pubs, murdering twenty-one people and injuring over two hundred.

The next day, a Northern Irish visitor calls at the Cronin's house. What will his arrival mean for Danny and where was the stranger on the night of the bombings?